R0083297226

06/2015

DISCARD

D1261370

CHRISTMAS IN LYREBIRD LAKE

Where Christmas miracles can *happen...*

For midwives Tara and Maeve, the sleepy town of Lyrebird Lake is the haven they've always wanted. So they're determined to make their first Christmas there special!

Neither of them are looking for love— but this year, with the help of some Lyrebird Christmas magic, the celebrations will be beyond their wildest imaginings...

You won't want to miss this fabulous new festive duet from Fiona McArthur:

MIDWIFE'S CHRISTMAS PROPOSAL

&

MIDWIFE'S MISTLETOE BABY

Dear Reader

I've loved Simon Campbell since he was a twenty-year-old on his first visit to Lyrebird Lake. That was about ten years ago in real time.

Simon has always made me smile, and has made me want to write his story for years. Readers have asked for him, and he's been in the back of my mind, but I just couldn't find the right woman for him—and he deserved the right woman.

Simon even visited in a couple of the Lyrebird Lake stories—a fleeting visit…just enough to remind me how much I cared about him, how much potential I always felt he had as a hero for the right woman. In the meantime he cared for his sisters, grew in his work, but always something was missing.

And then along came Tara… Tara who was so externally tough, so inwardly fragile, so able to be incredibly giving but so unskilled at relationships because she'd never had the chance. Tara who had missed out on so much in her childhood that only someone like Simon could hope to even the scales. Simon and the magic of Lyrebird Lake.

I've so enjoyed sharing with Tara and Simon in their journey to falling in love. I've loved the whole Christmas setting. I've loved revisiting the lyrebird dance. And I've absolutely *loved* setting a little of Maeve and Rayne's story amidst it all for the next book. I hope you do too.

Happy Christmas!

Fi xx

MIDWIFE'S CHRISTMAS PROPOSAL

BY
FIONA McARTHUR

First published in Great Britain 2014
by Mills & Boon, an imprint of Harlequin (UK) Limited,
Large Print edition 2015
Eton House, 18-24 Paradise Road,
Richmond, Surrey, TW9 1SR

ISBN: 978-0-263-25480-8

Harlequin (UK) Limited's policy is to use papers that are natural, renewable and recyclable products and made from wood grown in sustainable forests. The logging and manufacturing processes conform to the legal environmental regulations of the country of origin.

Printed and bound in Great Britain
by CPI Antony Rowe, Chippenham, Wiltshire

Mother to five sons, **Fiona McArthur** is an Australian midwife who loves to write. Mills & Boon® Medical Romance™ gives Fiona the scope to write about all the wonderful aspects of adventure, romance, medicine and midwifery that she feels so passionate about—as well as an excuse to travel! Now that her boys are older, Fiona and her husband, Ian, are off to meet new people, see new places, and have wonderful adventures. Fiona's website is at www.fionamcarthurauthor.com

Recent titles by Fiona McArthur:

CHRISTMAS WITH HER EX
GOLD COAST ANGELS: TWO TINY HEARTBEATS
THE PRINCE WHO CHARMED HER
A DOCTOR, A FLING & A WEDDING RING
SYDNEY HARBOUR HOSPITAL:
  MARCO'S TEMPTATION
FALLING FOR THE SHEIKH SHE SHOULDN'T
SURVIVAL GUIDE TO DATING YOUR BOSS
HARRY ST CLAIR: ROGUE OR DOCTOR?
MIDWIFE, MOTHER…ITALIAN'S WIFE
MIDWIFE IN THE FAMILY WAY
MIDWIFE IN A MILLION

These books are also available in eBook format from www.millsandboon.co.uk

Dedication

To my son Scott, who gifted me my first
parachute jump and the pictures that went with
it. And to the experience that I knew I would
put into this book.

And to Lawrence, my chute buddy
from Coffs Skydivers, who made it such fun
that I was never, ever scared.

Praise for
Fiona McArthur:

CHAPTER ONE

SIMON LOOKED AWAY from the road as he drove and across to his sister. Saw the tiny furrow in her brow even while she was sleeping. His eyes returned to the car in front. So she was still angry with him. Where had he gone wrong? All he'd ever wanted to do was protect his family. Protect Maeve from making the same mistakes their mother had made.

Maybe he felt more responsible than other siblings because the day he'd found out he was only a half-brother to Maeve and the girls had been devastating and he did wonder if he'd over-compensated.

But he was concerned about Maeve. About the way she'd been taken for a ride and she still couldn't see it. If Simon was honest with himself, he was just as hurt because he'd thought Rayne was his friend and he'd been suckered in as well. His sister's predicament had been all his fault.

Simon could feel his knuckles tighten on the wheel and he consciously relaxed them. He needed a holiday, and Maeve needed somewhere safe away from the baby's father if he ever came back, so maybe Lyrebird Lake was a good choice, like Maeve said.

And it was Christmas.

Two hours later they drove into the driveway of the Manse Medical Centre, Lyrebird Lake. The long day drive north from Sydney had been accomplished with little traffic issues or conversation. The last hour since they'd turned away from the coast had been unusually relaxing as they'd passed green valleys and bovine pedestrians. It was good to be here finally.

Simon felt that warmth of homecoming he'd

forgotten about in the rush and bustle of his busy life—almost like he could feel one of Louisa's enthusiastically warm hugs gearing up—as he slowed the car.

The engine purred to a stop and Maeve woke. She smiled sleepily, then remembered they were at odds with each other, and the smile fell away.

He watched her twist awkwardly in her seat as she took in the dry grass and huge gum trees 'I've heard such a lot about this place over the years. Thanks for bringing me, Simon.'

The tension in his shoulders lessened. At least she was talking to him again. He should never have mentioned his reservations about her idea of giving birth at Lyrebird Lake. That had been his obstetrician's point of view. Life had compartments, or should have, and he usually kept everything separate and in control.

Look what had happened when Maeve had lost control.

Simon's eyes travelled over the familiar

sights—the hospital and birth centre across the road from Louisa's house, the sleepy town just down the road, and the sparkling harp-shaped lake to the left behind the trees.

Unexpectedly, considering the mood he'd been in when he'd started out for here against his will, he couldn't do anything but smile as he eased his car under the carport at the side of the house.

'Curious.' Simon admired the old but beautifully restored Harley-Davidson tucked into a corner and then shrugged. He couldn't imagine Louisa on it but there were always interesting people staying at the manse.

It didn't seem ten years since he'd first come here with his new-found dad, Angus, but this big sprawling house Angus had brought him to all those years ago looked just the same. He'd arrived expecting awkwardness with his fledgling relationship with his birth father, and awkwardness staying with strangers in this small country town. But there hadn't been any.

He glanced at Maeve. 'Louisa will have heard us arrive.'

'Louisa used to be the housekeeper before she married your grandfather? Right?'

'Yep. They married late in life before he passed away. I stay with her when I come at Christmas.'

Simon climbed out quickly so he could open her door, but of course, Maeve was too darned independent. By the time they reached the path out front Louisa stood at the top of the steps, wiping her hands on her apron, and beamed one of Lyrebird Lake's most welcoming smiles.

Simon put his bag down and leapt up the two stairs to envelop the little woman in a hug. She felt just as roundly welcoming as he remembered. 'It's so good to see you, Louisa.'

'And you too, Simon. I swear you're even taller than last year.'

He had to smile at that as he stepped back. 'Surely I've reached an age where I can't keep growing.' He looked back at his sister, standing patiently at the bottom of the steps. 'Though with your cooking there is a possibility I could grow while I'm here.'

He offered a steadying hand but Maeve declined, made her way determinedly balancing her taut belly out front, as she climbed to the top of the stairs, so he guessed he wasn't totally forgiven.

He missed the easy camaraderie they used to have and hoped, perhaps a little optimistically, that Lyrebird Lake might restore that rapport as well. He guessed he had been out of line in some of the things he'd said about her choice in men and choice in birthing place.

'This is my youngest sister, Maeve. Maeve, this is my grandmother, Louisa.'

Louisa blushed with pleasure. 'You always were a sweetheart.' She winked at Maeve.

'Grandmother-in-law but very happy to pretend to be a real one.'

Maeve held out her hand. 'It's nice to finally meet you. Simon's told us a lot about you and everyone here. He says you're a wonderful cook.'

He saw Louisa's kind eyes brush warmly over Maeve and Simon relaxed even further. Of course Louisa would make them both feel wanted. 'Boys need their food.' He smiled to himself because he wasn't sure how he qualified for boy when he'd left thirty behind.

Louisa went on, 'You're very welcome here, dear,' as she glanced at Maeve's obvious tummy. 'It will be lovely to have a baby back in the house again, even if only for a wee while.'

Simon squeezed her plump shoulder. 'Dad and Mia not here?'

'They're coming over for dinner tonight. They thought it would be less overwhelming for Maeve if she had a chance to settle in first.'

She turned to Maeve. 'And we'll take it gradually to meet everyone else. There's a huge circle of family and friends who will want to catch up with Simon and meet you.'

Simon went back to pick up their bags and followed Louisa and Maeve into the house. The scent of cedar oil on the furniture made his nose twitch with memories—overlaid with the drifting promise of fresh-cut flowers and, of course, the tantalising aroma of Louisa's hot pumpkin scones.

His shoulders sagged as his tension lessened with each step he made into the house. He should have come here earlier. Leaving it until now had been crazy but his last two breech women had come in right at the last minute and he hadn't wanted to leave them uncertain about who would be there for them.

But enough. He needed to let go of work for a while and just chill, a whole month to Christmas and his first real break in years—and maybe the strain wasn't all on Maeve's side because he'd been holding on too tight for a while now.

This was what this place was good for. Finding the peace you were supposed to find as Christmas approached.

Behind a bedroom door in the same house Tara Dutton heard the car arrive and when, minutes later, footsteps sounded down the hall she rolled over in bed, yawned and squinted at the clock.

Two o'clock in the afternoon. She'd had six hours sleep, which was pretty good. Her mouth curved as she rolled back onto her back and stretched.

Last night's sharing of such a long, slow, peaceful labour and in the end a beautiful birth just as the sun had risen made everything shiny new. Babies definitely liked that time just before morning. Man, she loved this job.

She wriggled her toes and then sat up to swing her legs out of bed. Heard calm voices. Relief expanded, which was crazy when she didn't know them—but they were here safely. It would be Angus's son, Simon, and his sister. They arrived today and she admitted to a very healthy curiosity about the man everyone obviously adored, and even more so for his sister.

Simon's arrival had been the main topic of conversation for the last few days but Tara was more interested in Maeve.

Twenty-five, pregnant and a newly qualified midwife. Two out of three things Tara had been before she'd come here. Pregnancy wasn't on her agenda.

But that was okay. She breathed deeply and vowed again not to let the unchangeable past steal her present, and thankfully the calm she found so much easier to find in Lyrebird Lake settled over her like the soft quilt on her bed.

Clutching her bundle of fresh clothes, she opened the door to the hallway a crack to check the coast was clear, then scooted up the polished wooden floor to the bathroom and slipped inside.

Simon heard the bedroom door open from the kitchen and leaned back precariously in his chair until the two front legs were off the floor, and craned his neck to see who was in the hall. He glimpsed the back of a small, pertly bottomed woman in men's boxer shorts, one tiny red rose tattooed on her shoulder exposed by the black singlet as she disappeared into the bathroom.

His mouth curved as the years dropped away. He remembered arriving here with his father and their first sight of the woman who would later become his darling stepmother.

See! Always someone interesting staying in this place, he thought to himself again with a smile, and eased the front legs of the chair back on the floor.

* * *

When Tara stepped out of the bathroom thirty minutes later she felt nothing like the crumpled sleepyhead she'd been when she'd slipped in.

Her glance in the mirror over the claw-foot bath had reassured her. Blonde hair spikily fresh from the shower and her eyes confident and ready to meet the new guy and his intriguing sister.

Tara had experienced a lot of heartache and struggle in her life and it had made her wary of meeting new people. But the shadows of her past had made her who she was today—her T-shirt said it all: 'Woman With Attitude'.

As she walked back towards her room she passed the open door of one of the guest rooms. She couldn't help but have a tiny peek inside.

Simon's bag lay open on the bed, and she blinked at the neatly folded clothes in piles lined up in a row as she drew level, unlike her own 'bomb-hit' room, and she vowed she'd keep her door shut until he left.

Simon came into view, busily unpacking, and must have become aware of the eyes on him from the doorway. He glanced up, smiled, and she faltered. Man, that was some smile, like a warm breeze had blown down the hall and into her face, and Tara nearly tripped on the towel that slipped unexpectedly from her fingers.

'Hi, there. You must be Tara.'

She bent quickly to retrieve the towel. 'And you're Simon.' Tara moistened her lips. Louisa had said he was a bit of hunk like his dad but she'd put that down as favouritism for a relative. She certainly hadn't expected the fantasy that suddenly swirled in her head. Something like inviting him in two doors down for some seriously red-hot tumbling, but, *mamma mia,* he had a wicked bedroom grin.

Whoa, there, libido, where did you spring from? More to the point, where have you been?

Then he stepped closer and held out his hand and she forgot to think, just responded, and his fingers closed around hers, cool and surprisingly comforting, as he leaned forward with grace and unselfconscious warmth so that she couldn't be offended as he unexpectedly kissed her cheek.

'It's very nice to meet you.'

A cheek-kisser? Her brain clicked in. And nice to meet you, too, mister. There was nothing gushing or sleazy about the way he'd done the deed but she still wasn't quite sure how he managed to get away with it.

It was as if his whole persona screamed gentleman and usually the goody-two-shoes type turned her off. Though she was trying to change her tastes from bad boys to normal men after the last fiasco.

This guy made her think of one of those lifesavers on the beach at Bondi—tall, upstanding, with genuine love of humanity, careful of other people's safety but perfectly happy to risk their own lives to save yours. She blinked. And rumour said that apparently this guy wasn't even shackled to some discerning woman.

She was not bowled over! Not at all! She liked Angus for his solid dependability but this Simon beat his father hands down on the warmth stakes, that was all.

He was still waiting for her to answer him. Question? 'Nice to meet you, too.' What else could she say except something to get her out of his doorway? 'I'd better leave you to unpack.'

He didn't look like he wanted her to leave but she forced her feet to move. By the time she made it back to her bedroom her neck was hot with embarrassment. With great restraint she closed her door gently and with a sigh leant against it.

Talk about vibration. So much vibration it was lucky they hadn't spontaneously combusted. Holey dooley, she was in trouble if they were both going to live in this house for the next few weeks and react like that. Or maybe it was one-sided and he was totally oblivious to her. She smiled at her feet. Somehow she doubted it.

Simon watched her go. Couldn't help himself, really. Not a beauty in the stereotypical sense, her face was too angled for that, but she was a sassy, sexy little thing, and she had a definite pert little wiggle when she walked. She reminded him a bit of Maeve's girlfriends with that bolshie, I'm-my-own-woman persona that young females seemed to have nowadays.

Lord, he sounded like an old man but, seriously, this generation made him smile. But, then, didn't all women make him smile? Which might be why he hadn't seemed to find himself tied to just one. Problem with growing up with four sisters? Or problem with him and commitment?

Not that he didn't plan to have a family, settle down and be the best dad and husband he could be, but pledging to stay with one woman had been a tad difficult when he really didn't believe the odds of finding his other half.

Maybe he would end up in Lyrebird Lake at some stage, though after this last horror year he couldn't see himself taking the holistic approach to birth that was the norm here.

He turned back to the unpacking. Lined up the paired socks in the drawer and placed his folded jocks beside them. His last girlfriend had said his fussiness drove her mad and he was tempted to mess the line up a little but couldn't do it.

His sisters had always thought it hilarious that he liked things tidy. Having lived briefly with all of them as adults at one time or another, being the only sibling with stable housing, it wasn't such a bad thing. They were absolute disasters at order.

But he wouldn't change any of them. After his mother and stepfather had moved to America someone had needed to be able to put their hands on a spare house key to help out the current family member in crisis. And mild, acquired OCD wasn't a bad thing to have if you were a big brother—or a doctor. None of his patients had complained he was too careful.

He wondered what traits young Tara had acquired from her life and then shook his head. He didn't want to know. Lyrebird Lake was the last place to come for a fling because everyone would know before you'd even kissed her. A little startled at how easily he could picture that scenario, he brushed it away.

This was the place you brought one woman and settled down for good and he wasn't sure he believed in that for himself.

Five minutes later Tara had herself together enough to venture out to the kitchen, where Louisa had set out a salad for post-night-duty lunch.

The older lady hummed as she worked and the smile when she looked up to see Tara shone even brighter than normal.

'Have you met him?' No doubt at all whom she meant and Louisa wobbled with pride.

Tara had to smile. 'In the hallway.'

'Isn't he gorgeous?'

Tara picked up a carrot stick and took a bite. Chewed and swallowed—not just the carrot but the tiny voluptuous shiver as well. Back under control. 'He's very handsome. But no ideas, Louisa. He's an up-and-coming consultant here for a couple of weeks. And he's far too nice for me.'

'Silly girl. Of course he's not, he's just what you need.' She turned and started humming again and Tara had to smile as she glanced out the window to the veranda looking over the lake. She wasn't sure what that meant but she couldn't get offended by Louisa's mutterings—wouldn't do her any good if she did.

Tara had never had the kind of hugging acceptance she'd found in the small semi-rural community and sometimes she had to remind herself it might even be okay to learn to care for these people.

Then reality would resurface and she knew it would be just like the past—something would happen, she'd have to leave under a cloud and she'd be forgotten.

But she'd always have her work now wherever she went, she reminded herself, the first stability she'd known since the orphanage, and attainment had been such a golden rush as she'd passed her last exam, and that was priceless.

While socially she might be a bit stunted, okay, she granted more than a little stunted, but the work side of her life here couldn't be more satisfying with the midwifery-led birth centre.

She could finally do what she loved and, man, how she loved doing it. Loved the immersion in a woman's world of childbirth, the total connection as she supported a woman through her most powerful time, and then the exclusion when that woman departed for home. Just like a foster-family and she was good at saying goodbye. Except unlike where she'd done her training in the city, you bumped into the women again in Lyrebird Lake, and she wasn't quite used to that but it wasn't as bad as she'd thought it would be.

Technically she was autonomous in that she had her own women to care for, under the aegis of Montana, the most senior midwife, and they case-conferenced once a week so everyone knew what was going on. She was an integral part of the team of midwives and doctors who worked in the adjoining hospital as well on quiet days, and they were always happy to be back-up for any obstetric hiccough. So she felt supported in her role and that she contributed. It was a heady feeling and she still couldn't believe her luck.

Incredibly, everyone seemed as eager to learn

new trends as she was, and everyone researched changes in medical practice and then helped others to learn too. There was also enough going on in the other half of the hospital to stay updated on the medical side. This place was a utopia for a fledgling midwife who planned to make her career her life.

In the six months she'd been here her professional confidence had grown along with her belief in women and her own attending skills.

The motto of the lake, 'Listen to women,' had been gently but firmly reinforced. Very different from her training hospital's unwritten motto of 'We know best for all women.'

She wondered what the gorgeous Simon's philosophy was but coming from a busy practice working out of a major city hospital she had a fair suspicion.

Steady footsteps approached down the hallway and the object of her thoughts strolled into the room—which inexplicably seemed to shrink until he owned the majority of it—and she found herself basking in the warmth of his smile again.

Another unexpected flow of heat to the cheeks. Man, she'd never been a blusher. Thankfully, he turned the charm onto Louisa and Tara wilted back into her chair with relief.

She heard him say, 'I might go for a wander along the lake, Louisa, and relax after the drive.' He eased his neck as if it was kinked. 'Maeve's putting her feet up for an hour before this evening.'

Tara saw Louisa's eyes glint with determination and not being known for subtlety, Tara's stomach tightened, but it was too late. 'Why don't you join him, Tara? You always say it's good to walk after a night shift.'

CHAPTER TWO

Now, THAT WAS sink-into-the-floor-worthy. Tara could have glared at Louisa except the older lady didn't have a mean bone in her soft little body. Instead she shook her head. 'No. No. Simon will want to reacquaint himself. He doesn't need me to hold his hand.'

'I won't hold your hand if you don't want me to,' he was teasing, but this time there was no hiding the connection and she closed her eyes.

When she opened them he was smiling quizzically at her, and grudgingly she accepted that as a recipient it didn't feel as bad as it could have.

'I don't bite,' he said. 'I'd like the company but only if you want to.'

Growth experience. He thinks you're a socially adept woman. That would be a first. She could do this. The guy worked with women all the time. Practise at least on a man who was skilled at putting women at ease. Made sense. 'Fine. I can't feel more embarrassed.' She glanced at Louisa, who apparently didn't bat an eyelid at putting her in the hot seat and was humming happily, satisfied two of her chickens were getting along.

She could almost smile at that. Tara picked up the sunglasses she'd left beside the window because she still suffered from that night-duty glare aversion that too little sleep left you with. Simon held the door open for her—something that happened a lot in the quaintness around here. A few months ago she would have been surprised but today she just murmured, 'Thank you,' and passed in front of him.

They'd turned out of the driveway before he spoke and surprisingly the silence wasn't awkward. Thank goodness someone else didn't mind peace and quiet. Years of keeping her own counsel had taught her the value of quiet time—but quiet time in the company of others was an added bonus she could savour. She didn't think she'd met anyone she felt so in tune with so quickly. Though the air might be peaceful, it still vibrated between them.

Stop worrying, she admonished herself, a habit she'd picked up in the orphanage and on foster-parent weekends. Just let it be.

She looked ahead to where the path curled around the edge of the lake like a pale ribbon under the overhanging trees, and the water shimmered through the foliage like diamonds of blue glass in the ripples.

This place soothed her soul more than she could have ever imagined it would. Until unexpectedly a creature rustled in the undergrowth and her step faltered as it swished away from them into the safety of the water's edge. Typical, she thought, there's always a snake in the grass.

She shuddered. Snakes were the only crea-
tures she disliked but that was probably because
someone had put one in her bed once. 'Hope
that wasn't something that can bite.'

Simon glanced after the noise. 'No. Doubt it.
Might even have been a lyrebird.' He grinned.
'Have they told you about the legend of the lyrebird?' There was definitely humour in his deep
voice. The man had a very easy soothing bass
and she found herself listening more to the mel-
ody of the words than the content. Tried harder
for the words.

'Nope. You mean as in why they call the place
Lyrebird Lake?' She shrugged. 'Not really into
legends.' Or fairy-tales. Or dreams of gorgeous
men falling in love with her and carrying her
off. Pshaw. Rubbish.

'Ah. A disbeliever.' He nodded his head sagely
and she had to smile at his old-fashioned quaintness. 'So you wouldn't believe that in times of
stress or, even more excitingly, when you meet

your true love, a real live lyrebird appears and dances for you.'

Now she knew he was laughing at her. She rolled her eyes. 'Well, I haven't seen one and I've been here six months.'

'Me either. And I've been coming here off and on for ten years.' The smile was back in his voice. 'But my father and Mia have.'

This time her brows rose and she had no doubt her healthy dollop of scepticism was obvious. 'Really.'

His eyes crinkled. 'And Montana and Andy. And Misty and Ben.'

'You're kidding me.' These were sane, empowering people she'd looked up to. Consultants and midwives. Icons of the hospital. Or maybe he was pulling her leg. 'Don't believe you.'

'Nope. All true.' His eyes were dancing but she could see he was telling the truth as he believed it.

Then he'd been conned. 'How many times has this happened?'

He shrugged. 'Don't know. You'd have to ask.'

Brother. 'I will.' She shook her head. He'd probably just made it all up. Men did say weird things to impress women. Though he didn't seem like one of those guys, but, then again, her sleaze detection system had never worked well. 'What else don't I know about this place?'

He glanced around. 'Well, half of that hill behind the lake...' he pointed across the water '...is full of disused gold mines and labyrinths of old tunnels crisscross underneath our feet.'

She looked down at the path and grimaced. Imagined falling through into an underground cavern. She'd always had claustrophobia— or had since one particular foster-sibling had locked her in a cupboard. Now, that wasn't a pleasant thought. 'Thanks for that. How to ruin a walk.'

'Well, not really under our feet. That might be

stretching it a bit far. But certainly all around the hillside and a long way this way.'

'Okay.' She shook off the past and thought rationally about it. 'I guess half our hospital's business comes from the mines out of town so it makes sense we'd have some here.' She glanced at him as they walked at a steady pace around the lake. Maybe she could start fossicking for gold after work—above ground, of course—and make her fortune to pay off the debts Mick had left her with. 'Have you been in them?'

He laughed. Even looked a little pink-cheeked. 'Once. To my embarrassment.' Shook his head at himself. 'I can't believe I brought this up.' He glanced at Tara ruefully and sighed. 'I had to ring Mia to get my dad to rescue me.'

She looked across at him and grinned. Good to see other people did dumb things. 'Ouch.'

'Not one of my more glorious moments.'

She looked at him, loose-limbed, strongly muscled with that chiselled jaw and lurking smile. A man very sure of his world and his place in it. She wished. Shook her head. 'I'm sure you have enough glorious moments.'

The quizzical look was back but all he said was, 'Yep. Hundreds.'

She had to laugh at that. 'I'm still waiting for mine.'

'My turn not to believe you.' So he'd noticed her scepticism. He tilted his head and studied her with leisurely thoroughness. 'Do you enjoy your work?'

'Love it.'

'Then I'll bet you have lots of successes too.'

She thought about earlier that morning and smiled. 'I do get to share other women's glorious moments.' Changed the subject. 'Mia says you're running a breech clinic at Sydney Central?'

'Yep. Was converted by an amazing guy I worked with when I was a registrar. Had the motto "Don't interfere". Said most women had the ground work for a normal breech birth.'

She couldn't agree more but her training hospital hadn't subscribed to that theory. The only babies allowed to be born in the breech position were the ones who came in off the street ready to push their own way out. She'd never been lucky enough to be on duty for that. 'I've watched a lot of breech births on videos but I haven't seen one in real life.'

'You will. Hopefully trends are changing with new research. Women are demanding a chance at least. Maybe one of your glorious moments is coming up. You obviously love midwifery.'

'I was always going to be a nurse, because my mother was a nurse, even though I don't remember much about her, but then one of my friends lost a baby and I decided I'd be a midwife. It was a good decision.'

'I think it's a fabulous decision. Some of my best friends are midwives.' He returned to their previous conversation. 'But I can't believe there isn't more to your life than your job.'

'You're right.' She thought of her arrival here six months ago. 'I love my bike.'

'Ah. So the black monster is yours?'

'Yep. The sum total of my possessions.'

'University can be expensive.'

She'd only just started paying that back. It was the bills Mick had run up all over town that crippled her. More fool her for having the lease and the accounts in her name. They'd both been in the orphanage together and when she'd met him again she'd been blinded to his bitter and dangerous side because, mistakenly, she'd thought she'd found family.

But her dream of everything being fair and equal had been torn into a pile of overdue notices. 'Druggie boyfriends can be expensive too.' Unintentionally the words came out on a sigh. What the heck was she doing?

'Nasty. Had one of those, did you.'

She turned her face and grimaced at the lake so he couldn't see. She was tempted to say 'Dozens' but it wasn't true. It had taken her too long to actually trust someone that first time. 'Hmm. I'm a little too used to people letting me down. Don't usually bore people with it.'

'Don't imagine you bore people at all.'

She could hear the smile in his voice and some of the annoyance with herself seeped away then surged again, even though it was unreasonably back towards Simon. What would he know about where she'd been? What she'd been through?

Then, thankfully, the calmness she'd been practising for the last six months since she'd met these people whispered sense in her ear and she let the destructive thoughts go. Sent the whole mess that was her past life out over the rippled water of the lake and concentrated on the breath she eased out.

She had no idea where the conversational ball

lay as she returned to the moment but let that worry go too. Took another breath and let her shoulders drop.

'That's some control you have there, missy.'

She blinked at Simon and focussed on him. On his calm grey eyes mainly and the warmth of empathy—not ridicule, as she'd expected, but admiration and understanding.

'I'm practising positive mindfulness and self-control.' She didn't usually tell people that either.

He nodded as if he knew what it was, probably didn't, then he surprised her with his own disclosure. 'I'm not good at it. But if it makes you feel any better I have hang-ups too. Luckily I have a very busy work life.'

She smiled at the statement. 'Funny how we can hide in that. I was studying like mad, paying bills for two in my time off, and he was gambling and doing drugs when I thought he was at uni.' She shrugged it away. 'Now I have a busy work life and a really big bike.'

'The bike's a worry.'

'The bike?' She shook her head and could almost feel the wind on her face and the vibration in her ears. 'Not if you have no ties. Always loved the spice of danger. It would be different if I had someone who needed me.' There was a difference between someone needing you and someone using you. She'd agreed not to drag them both through the court system but she would only keep all the bills at the cost of his bike. Even though it had only been worth a quarter of the debts he'd run up, possession of the bike had restored some of her self-esteem. Mick hadn't been happy and sometimes she wondered if it really all was finished.

'Ah. So you admit that motorbikes are the toys of possibly "temporary" citizens?'

'Spoken like a true doctor.'

'Ask any paramedic. The stats are poor.'

She grinned at him—he had no idea. 'But the fun is proportional. I could take you for a ride one day.'

He raised his brows. 'I'd have to think about that.'

'Sure. No rush. You have time.' She couldn't imagine him ever saying yes. Which was a good thing because she suspected the experience of Simon's arms wrapped around her and his thighs hard up against her backside would make it very difficult to concentrate. Instead she looked up ahead. 'So how far are we walking? You'll be at your father's house soon.'

He glanced up in surprise. Looked around. 'You're right. I guess he'll be at work anyway.'

'Mia will be home. She was on duty the night before me.'

'I'd forgotten you were up all night.' His glance brushed warmly over her and surprisingly she didn't feel body-conscious. It wasn't that kind of look. 'You do it well. I always look like a dishrag for the next few days.'

She nodded wisely. 'That would be the age factor.'

It was his turn to blink then grin, and she was glad he had a sense of humour. Nice change. Not sure why she'd tried to alienate him, unless she'd wanted him to turn away so she wouldn't have to.

'*Touché*, young woman.' He looked ahead to the house they were approaching. 'Let's go and see my gorgeous step-mama and my second family of sisters. This old man needs a cold drink.'

CHAPTER THREE

SIMON'S STEP-MAMA, NOT all that much older than Simon, greeted them with open arms, her red curls bouncing as she rushed out to hug him. Her eyes sparkled as she stared up at Simon fondly, and Tara was pretty sure nobody had ever looked at her like that.

Two copper-curled miniature Mias tumbled out of the door, one more demurely because she was eleven, and the other squealing because she was eight, but in the end both threw themselves at Simon, who scooped them up one in each hand and spun them around as he hugged them. 'How are my little sisters today?'

Tara unobtrusively admired the stretch of material over his upper arms as with impressive ease he twirled the girls like feathers. He might be way out of her league but this Simon Campbell was certainly delicious eye candy. She could deal with just looking in. She did that all the time.

He kissed them both on the cheek and they giggled as he put them down.

'It feels like ages since we saw you, Simon.' The elder girl, Layla, pouted.

'Eleven months. Christmas.' He put them at arm's length and looked them over, nodded, satisfied they looked well, before he turned back and studied Mia again. 'And how is my gorgeous step-mama?'

'All the better for seeing you.' They embraced again and the genuine warmth overflowed to where Tara was standing. 'Once a year is not enough.'

Touchy-feely family or what! Tara pushed away the tiny stab of jealousy. So what if Simon had this whole network of adoring relatives and she didn't.

Simon grinned and stepped back so that Mia turned to Tara and leaned in for a hug. Tara tried, she really did, to hug back. She seemed to be getting better at it. 'Tara. Great to see you, too.' Mia nodded her head at Simon. 'So you two have met.'

Simon grinned. 'In the hallway. Made me think of you and Dad. Then Louisa nagged Tara into accompanying me on my walk.'

'Poor Tara.' Mia grinned and looked at her. 'Met in the hallway, did you? I hope you had clothes on, Tara. I was in a towel when I met his father and sparks flew even on the first day.'

Tara had to laugh. 'In that case I'm glad to say I was dressed. And had six hours' sleep under my belt.'

Mia's eyes sharpened. 'That's right. You were on night duty last night. How was Julie's labour? What time was her baby born?'

'Quarter to five this morning, on the dot. Sunrise.'

Mia shook her head with a smile. 'Babies seem to love sunrise.'

'I was just thinking that.' Tara soaked up the warmth she was getting used to from these people and then blinked as Mia spun on her heel. 'Come in. What was I thinking?' She waved a hand. 'Have a cold drink. Angus will be jealous I got to see you first, Simon.'

'But not surprised.'

Mia laughed. Then she sobered as she remembered. 'Anyway, how are you? You look tired. And how is Maeve?'

'I'm fine. Maeve's pregnancy has four weeks to go and the baby's father is still in a US penitentiary. I hope.'

'I'm sorry you've all had that worry. What did your mother say? It must be hard for her to be living so far away in Boston when her daughter is pregnant.'

'There's not a lot she can do. Maeve refuses

to have her baby in America and Dad's unwell and Mum can't leave.'

'Then Maeve is lucky she has you.'

He shrugged. 'My youngest sister has me stumped the way she is at the moment. I can't say anything right. I'm worried about her.'

Tara wasn't quite sure if she was supposed to hear all this or whether she should drift away and look out the window over the lake or something, but she guessed everyone else would know the ins and out of it. She'd find out eventually.

Mia was talking and walking until she opened the fridge. 'So you could've brought her here earlier, even if you couldn't get away. She could have stayed here or with Louisa. You know how Louisa loves to have people under her roof. And Tara's there.' She turned to Tara and drew her back into the circle.

'Isn't that right, Tara?'

'I've never felt more welcome in my life,' she said quietly, and hoped the others missed the pathetic neediness in the statement.

Thankfully they must have because Simon went on as if all was normal. 'Well, now that I'm here I'm hoping I can manage a few weeks of relaxation till she settles in. Though I may have to do a quick trip back and forth in the middle. It depends when my next two private women go into labour, but they're not due till after the new year.'

Mia closed the refrigerator and returned with two tall glasses of home-made lemonade. 'So how are your training sessions going? Have you managed to inspire a few more docs to think breech birth without Caesarean can be a normal thing?'

He took the glass. 'Thanks. 'I'm trying. My registrar's great.' He took a sip and closed his eyes in delight. 'Seriously, Mia, you could retire on this stuff.'

She actually looked horrified. 'Retire? Who wants to retire?'

'Sometimes I think I do,' Simon said half-jokingly, and Mia raised her brows.

The concern was clear in her voice. 'You sound like your father when I first met him. You do need a break. Watch out or Angus will be nagging you to move here and set up practice.'

'Haven't completed the research I want to do. A few years yet.'

A vision of Simon with a wife and kids popped unexpectedly into Tara's mind. Made it a bit of a shame she didn't stay in places too long, then she realised where her thoughts were heading. That way lay disappointment. Didn't she ever learn? She'd rather think about Maeve. 'So has Maeve joined any parenting classes?'

Simon shook his head and his concern was visible. 'Wouldn't go to classes in Sydney.'

Tara shrugged. 'I don't think that's too weird.

She's a midwife. She knows the mechanics. And sometimes women don't want to think about labour until right at the end. Or be involved in the couples classes without a partner. I get that.'

She could feel Mia's eyes on them and obviously she wanted to say something. Tara waited. Mia was very cool and worth listening to.

'Why don't you ask her if she'd like to be on your caseload, Tara? I think a younger midwife would help when she's feeling a bit lost and lonely.'

Tara could feel her chest squeeze with the sudden shock of surprise. That was pretty big of Mia to trust a family member to her. Her eyes stung and she looked away. Nobody had ever treated her as she was treated here. Or trusted her. She just hoped she didn't let them down. 'You know I'd love to. But I guess it depends who she wants.'

Simon looked at Mia too. He felt the shock and turned to look at his stepmother. He wasn't sure what he thought about that and saw Mia nod reassuringly. Someone else looking after Maeve, not Mia? He looked at the bolshie but sincere young woman beside him. Was she experienced enough? What if something went wrong?

Then saw the flare of empathy for his sister in Tara's face and allowed the reluctant acceptance that Mia could be right. Maeve wanted to run the show. Wanted to listen to her body without interference, if he'd listened at all to the arguments they'd had over the last couple of weeks, and he had no doubt young Tara was holistic enough for his sister to be able to do that.

Normally he would be right there with a woman, cheering her on, but he was having serious personal issues doing that with the sister he had felt most protective of all his life. Not that he'd actually be there, of course. But he was darned sure he'd be outside the door, pacing.

So maybe Mia was right. It could be harder

for Maeve to relax with the connection so strong between her brother and his stepmother.

He found the words out in the air in front of him before he realised. 'We'll see what she says.'

He reassured himself that if Mia didn't have faith in Tara, she wouldn't have suggested it. And despite the mixed feelings he was starting to have about this intriguing young woman he really did feel a natural confidence in her passion for her work.

He'd seen it before. How Lyrebird Lake could bring out the best in all of them. Maybe he had lost that since he'd been so immersed in the high-tech, high-risk arena of obstetrics he studied now.

He'd even seen it with his own father. From hotshot international evacuation medic to relaxed country GP.

Maeve and Tara did have a lot in common and would get on well, the dry voice in his head agreed—all the way to dropkicking past boy-friends!

No. It would be good. This was all going to turn out even better than he'd hoped.

CHAPTER FOUR

THE DINNER PARTY was a reasonable success. Maeve smiled and said the right things but still kept her distance and seemed a little flat to Simon. His stepmother was her own gorgeous self and treated both young women as if they were long-term friends of hers, and his father said very little but smiled every time his eyes rested on his wife or daughters.

Louisa was in her element because she loved dinner parties and seeing the family together. She was always happiest when children were around.

And young Tara, dressed in skin-tight, very stressed jeans that showed glimpses of skin beneath the ragged material moulded to her lush little body, drew his eyes like a magnet every time she walked past to the fridge on some errand for Louisa.

His father came to stand beside him. 'Mia says you seem to get on well with Tara.'

'She's easy to get along with.'

Tara laughed at something Louisa whispered as she walked past again with a platter of fruit for dessert and both men sneaked a glance.

Angus looked away first. 'I think our Tara's had an interesting life. She's a tough little cookie, on the outside at least.'

Simon glanced at his father's face. 'Lots of people have tough lives.'

'Guess so.' Angus took a sip of his beer. 'What happened to Julia?'

'Didn't work out. Said I didn't pay her enough attention. Let my work come between us.'

'Did you?'

'Maybe.' Simon thought about it. 'Definitely. Spent a lot of time apologising for leaving and heading into work. Started to enjoy work more than home and she found another guy.'

'Took me a while to find Mia. It will happen to you one day and you'll recognise it.'

They both looked at Angus's wife. 'If I find a woman like Mia I'll be very happy.'

'Would you settle here?'

'So this is a job interview?'

'Cheeky blighter. Would you?'

'Not yet. But in the future I'm not ruling it out.'

Angus nodded then added innocently, 'Can you do three days for me, starting Monday?'

Simon laughed. 'I knew this was leading somewhere. Why?'

'Seeing as you're here, and Mia's had a big birthday last week, I thought I might take her up to Brisbane to do Christmas shopping. She loves it. Take her and the girls for a mini-holiday.'

Simon laughed. 'Can't see you shopping with Christmas music in the background.'

He grimaced. 'It's only a couple of days. I'm

going to sit back and watch my women. Need more of that when you get to my age.'

'Poor old man.'

'Absolutely. So, will you?'

Simon had done the occasional shift in the small hospital over the last few years when one of the senior partners had had to go away, and he'd enjoyed most of the small-town country feel of it. Angus knew that. 'Sure. Why not? Andy will be point me in the right direction if needed. Haven't done much general medicine for a few years, though.'

'You've got a young brain. You'll manage. And it's almost December. Louisa wants the decorations up.'

Simon laughed. 'Thanks. And no doubt you'll bring her back something new I'll have to assemble.'

Tara walked past again and Simon's eyes followed. Angus bit his lip and smiled into his drink.

* * *

The next morning Tara heard Simon go out not long after daylight. It would be pleasantly cool before the heat of the day, she thought as she pulled her sheet up, the blanket having been discarded on the floor, and she wondered drowsily where he was going.

And then, as her fantasies drifted, wondered what he was wearing, wondered if he wore his collar open so she'd see his lovely strong neck and chest. Funny, that—she'd never had a throat fetish before.

She grinned to herself and snuggled down further. Nice make-believe. And Mia was amazing. They all were, and yesterday, as far as Tara was concerned, had been an intriguing insight into the Campbell family and Simon in particular.

Watching the dynamics between Simon and his father had been fascinating. She certainly looked at Angus differently after some of the exploits Mia had mentioned. Who would have known?

She'd never seen such equal footing between father and son but, then, her experience was limited to snatches of dysfunctional family life. Maybe it was because Simon had made it to twenty before he'd even met his biological father. Angus was certainly proud of him and the feeling looked to be mutual. And both of them obviously adored Mia and the girls.

She'd have felt a bit like the Little Match Girl looking in the Christmas window if it hadn't been for Maeve, who, despite looking like she'd just stepped out of a fashion magazine, had looked more lost than she had. Why was that?

Maeve was who she should be concentrating her thoughts on. Especially if she agreed to join Tara's caseload.

An hour later she wandered down to the kitchen and Maeve, immaculate in designer maternity wear and perfectly made up, was there, picking at a piece of toast as if she wanted to eat it one crumb at a time. Perhaps her pregnancy hormones still gave her nausea in the mornings. Tara had seen lots of women like that well into their last trimester of pregnancy.

'Morning, all.' Friendly but not too pushy, she included Maeve and Louisa in her smile as she sat down. Louisa liked to fuss and judging by the tension in the room Maeve didn't appreciate it.

'Hello, dear.' Louisa cast her a relieved glance. 'What are you doing today?'

'Have a young mums' class this afternoon but happy to do whatever if you need something, Louisa.'

'No. I'm off to bingo with a friend down at the hall and I wondered if you and Maeve could fix your own lunches.'

'No problem.' She smiled at the younger woman. 'We'll manage, won't we, Maeve?'

The girl barely looked up. 'Of course.'

'Still nauseous?' Tara could see she looked a little pale around the cheeks.

Maeve grimaced. 'Getting worse, not better. And I'm starting to get this insane itch that's driving me mad.'

Tara frowned. A tiny alarm pinged in her brain with the symptoms but she let it lie for a moment. 'Not fun. What have you tried?'

'Pretty well everything.' She shrugged. 'Pressure-point armbands. Ginger. Sips of cold water. Sips of hot water for nausea.' She absently scratched her belly through her shirt. 'And just calamine for the itch but I only put it on the places you can't see. I never liked pink as a kid and it's too embarrassing to be painted pink all over.'

Tara laughed. 'That's the thing with midwives. We know all the things we tell other women and it sucks when it doesn't work.'

'Embarrassing really.' The young woman

looked a little less tense now that Tara had acknowledged Maeve knew her stuff.

'I imagine being pregnant would expand your thirst for remedies?'

Maeve rolled her eyes and even smiled. 'You have no idea. I've read everything I can find on common complaints of pregnancy.'

'I'll have to get you to brush me up on them later.'

Tara was glad to hear that Maeve really did have a sense of humour. 'Makes you wonder what the women thought when it didn't work for them either.' They smiled at each other.

Maeve nodded. 'I'll clarify next time. Works *most* of the time.'

'Have you had a chance to sit down with someone and talk about the actual plans you have for labour?'

It was a reasonable question, considering she'd just moved to a new centre for care, but Tara felt the walls go up from across the table.

Maeve shot her a glance. 'You mean antenatal classes? Simon been talking to you?'

'I'm guessing Simon talks to everyone.' A little bit ambiguous. 'But Mia asked, yes. I usually run a younger mums' class this week and I thought seeing as you were a midwife you might be interested in helping me—from a pregnant woman's perspective. But, then, you might prefer the idea of just a chat, and I'd be happy to do that if you did want one if you're not already teed up with someone else?'

'Sorry. I'm just a bit narky lately. Everything is a mess.'

Life. Didn't she know it could do that! 'Oh, yeah. It gets like that sometimes. I'm an expert at it. Plus your itch and nausea would impact on anyone's day, let alone someone carrying a watermelon everywhere.'

Maeve did laugh then. 'Feels like it. And it feels like this pregnancy is never going to end, but I'm going to be patient and not let anyone push me into something I don't want.'

'Good on you. Who were you thinking of seeing here?'

Maeve shrugged. 'Don't know. As long as it's low key I don't care. I saw the doctor Simon teed me up with a few times but last month he started talking about induction of labour and possible epidurals and maybe even Caesareans. I couldn't believe it, so I told Simon I was out of there. He wouldn't hear of a home birth and we compromised on Lyrebird Lake Birth Centre.'

'And the father of the child?'

Maeve looked away. 'Conspicuous by his absence. And I don't want to look back on this birth and regret it. I'm already regretting enough about this pregnancy. I need to have some control and I wasn't going to get it at Simon's hospital.'

Tara was a hundred per cent agreeable to that. 'Go, you, for standing up for yourself and your baby.' Tara wondered if she could offer without putting too much pressure on her.

'There's three doctors here who do antenatal care, and four midwives. If you think you'd be happy on a midwifery programme, you just need to pick someone. I've two women due in the next fortnight but apart from home visits I'm free to take on new women. You could meet the other midwives tomorrow but keep it in mind. You're probably due for tests around now anyway.'

Maeve looked across and smiled with a shyness Tara guessed was way out of character. 'Actually, that would be great.'

'You sure?'

Maeve looked relieved. 'Very. And we can talk about the labour then too.'

'Fine. We'll wander down to the clinic after morning tea, check you and baby out, and get all the papers sorted with the stuff you brought. If you change your mind after I've nosed my way through your medical and social history I can hand you on to someone else.'

'Lord. Social history. And isn't all that a disaster? Sometimes I feel like I'll never get sorted. I never used to be like this.'

'Sympathy.' Tara smiled in complete agreement. 'I was pretty lost before I came here. The good news is that you're female so you'll still come out on top.'

Maeve blinked and then smiled. 'Okay, then. Must remember that for my clever brother.'

'He seems nice.'

'Too nice.' Both girls looked at each other, were obviously thinking of their previous boyfriends who had been anything but, and laughed. Ten seconds later they heard footsteps leaping up the back stairs and Simon appeared behind the back porch screen door. Of course both of them struggled to control their mirth.

'What's so funny?' The door shut quietly behind him and he looked from one to the other, brows raised, fine sweat across his brow. Obviously he'd been running.

'Nothing.' In unison.

He shook his head at them. 'Okay. Girl talk. You want to go for a swim, Maeve?'

Tara saw her face change. Become shuttered. 'No, thanks. I'm catching up on my emails.'

'Tara?'

She could just imagine Simon in swimmers. Wouldn't she just. 'No, thanks.'

'You sure?'

Maeve chimed in. 'Go. It's your day off. We can do that other thing when you come back. There's hours before then.'

Tara didn't understand the wall Maeve had erected between herself and her brother. If she had a brother like Simon she'd be all over him, but there was probably stuff she didn't know. 'Fine. Thanks. I love to swim.' She looked at him. Saw him glance at his watch. 'I'm guessing you want to go now?'

Simon nodded and he seemed happy enough that she'd agreed to come. She'd hate to think all these people were forcing her on him but what the heck. She'd enjoy it while it lasted.

'Five minutes enough time? Out the front?' he said.

'I'll be there.'

Simon watched Tara towel her shoulders vigorously and then rub shapely calves and stand on one leg and dry her toes.

He suffered a brief adolescent urge to metamorphose into her towel. Apart from her delightful breasts her body was firm and supple and he suspected she would feel incredibly sleek and smooth in his arms.

The swim had proved to a little more bracing than they'd both expected and he saw her shiver. He guessed she'd had a cold start. 'Sorry. I was hot from my run so it feels good to me.'

She shrugged. 'Hey, it's summer in Queensland. I can swim all year round.' The idea was sound but the rows of goose-bumps covering both arms and her delightful thighs made Simon want to bring her in close and warm her against his chest.

Or maybe it wasn't the goose-bumps he wanted to warm against him. It had been a while since the last time he'd noticed so much about a woman. Passing glances, inner appreciation, sure, but this little firebrand had him constantly ready without any effort on her part. Danger. Alert.

Thankfully she remained oblivious to his shift in thoughts. That was a good thing.

He could see her mind was still on the swim. 'And Lyrebird Lake's too far south for crocodiles.'

Crocodiles. Now, there's a thought. He'd bet she wasn't afraid of any animal. 'Not sure why but I get the feeling it would take more than a crocodile to scare you off something you wanted to do.'

She grinned at him and that was an added bonus. Her whole face lit up and warmed him more than any towel could. 'Thank you, kind sir. I'll take that as a compliment.'

'It was.' And a bit of a surprise. He didn't usually go for the daredevil type. 'So you have an interesting bucket list?'

'I've always wanted to go skydiving. Birthday present for myself next week.'

Of course she was. 'Seriously?'

'Yep.' Her eyes shone at the thought.

Well it was the last thing he wanted to do. 'Birthday wish I wouldn't be keen on.'

She shook her head and her spiky hair flicked droplets around like a little sparkler. 'They say you're never the same after you do it. All to do with my belief to live life so I know that I've been here before I leave this earth.' She looked so intense when she said that. There was something incredibly gloomy about such a vibrant young woman contemplating her mortality that chilled him.

'You planning to leave this world?'

She shrugged. 'Not planning to, but anything can happen. My dad and mum died when I was six. That's why I'm always glad when people driving arrive safely. I was made a ward of the state. I grew up in an orphanage.'

'I'm sorry about your parents.' Hard reality to face at that age. At any age. 'What about her mother? Your grandmother?'

'Died in childbirth. No siblings.' No expression. No plea for sympathy. And he was guessing not much childhood—which explained a lot. But there was a wall that said as good as a raised hand, 'Don't give me any sympathy.'

'Nasty family history.' Understatement. He seriously wasn't being flippant. It was a shocker and he could see how that could be a trigger for more risky, adventurous behaviour. 'My life is boring in comparison.'

'Tell me about boring.'

He shrugged. 'Nothing to tell except my mother didn't tell my biological father she was pregnant, a minor glitch I didn't find out about till after I grew up. That was as adventurous as I got.'

'That's adventurous. Especially searching him out as an adult.' There was wistfulness in her eyes when she said that and he knew she wished she had someone to search out. He'd never actually looked at it like that.

'So, anyway, maybe I should be up for exciting escapades.' His voice trailed off as she pulled her T-shirt over her head and it stuck, alluringly, in a few damp places.

He closed his mouth and glanced away. Regathered his thoughts with some difficulty. 'One day I will try being adventurous for a change.'

She looked him up and down and he sucked

in his belly. Not that he was ashamed of his six pack, and not quite sure why he should even think about it because he wasn't usually a vain man, but he had no control over the reflex. She just did that to him.

'You could jump with me on Tuesday if you like.'

He knew the horror showed on his face.

To make it worse, then she laughed at him. And not even with him. Not sure he liked that either.

Tough. He wasn't jumping. 'How about I come and be ground support? Hold a glass of champagne for you.'

He could see she liked the idea of that and he felt he'd redeemed himself somewhat. 'Thank you. That'd be very cool.'

'Okay. We'll talk about it later when I get the picture out of my mind of you stepping out of a perfectly good plane.' They picked up the towels and walked back towards the path.

'So what were you and Maeve talking about doing later?'

'Antenatal clinic. I offered and she's accepted to go on my caseload.' She sounded a little hesitant and he guessed it could be confronting to take on the sister of the consultant. He needed Maeve to see someone and he didn't have much chance of her listening to him at the moment.

'That's great. Really. I think you guys will have a great rapport.'

She flashed a grateful glance at him. 'Thanks, Simon. I'm looking forward to it. I'll take good care of her.'

CHAPTER FIVE

THE ANTENATAL CLINIC opened at eleven a.m. seven days a week. That way the morning midwife had discharged any women and babies who were due to go home. Plus the ward was often less busy so the women booking in could look around. Except when there was a woman in labour.

Tara had ten women on her caseload at the moment in various stages of pregnancy and two who had already delivered on the six-week postnatal check programme.

The first visit at least would be held at the clinic but most visits she would do at the woman's home. All the midwives took turns to carry the maternity phone in case one of the other midwives needed help in the birthing suite or two women went into labour at once on the same midwife's caseload.

Maeve looked very interested in the running of the unit, judging by the way her head never stopped swivelling, and Tara smiled quietly to herself. She'd bet there'd be some thought about staying on after Maeve's baby was born.

Even during the antenatal check Maeve was asking questions about the way they ran the caseloads, and the girls were firm friends by the time the official paperwork was completed.

Tara sat back. 'Okay. So your blood pressure is slightly elevated and your baby is a little under the normal size for thirty-six weeks but all of those things could be normal. It's nothing startling but we've done a couple of extra blood tests to rule out anything we need to watch for.'

'You thinking my blood pressure could go up more? So watch out for toxaemia?'

'We'll both have a good look at the results. At the moment you feel well in yourself, and baby is moving nicely, but I wonder about the nausea and the itch.' She looked at her. 'Don't you?'

'Yeah.' Maeve sighed. 'Of course I'm thinking it could need watching. That's why I'm glad we sorted out the caseload. In case Simon decided I was high risk and whisked me back to Sydney.'

'If you got a lot worse we are a low-risk unit. But being thirty-six weeks helps so we don't have to deal with a premature baby if things did escalate.'

'Don't tell Simon.'

Tara had wondered if this would come. 'If Simon asks, I'm not going to lie.'

'And if he doesn't ask, don't tell him.'

'As long as the tests come back normal, there's nothing to talk about. Sure.'

'You wiggling out of that?'

'You asking me for the impossible?' Tara countered, and she saw the realisation in Maeve's eyes that she wasn't a pushover. She couldn't be.

Maeve stood up and so did Tara. It was going to go one way or the other.

'Fine.' Maeve shook her head. 'Sorry. I don't know why Simon makes me so wild. He hasn't done anything wrong. I guess it's because I feel like I let him down when I made the choices I did.'

'Choices are there to be made and who knows what the end result will be? But, boy, do I know that feeling.' She handed Maeve her antenatal card. 'I'm trying to learn that blame and guilt are useless emotions. So is resentment. It's helped me. Hard to do but letting all that go has really made me start each day fresh.'

Maeve patted her stomach. 'A bit hard when the reminder is poking out in front.'

'Nah. Perfect time to be fresh with a new baby. I'll be there for your birth, Louisa will spoil you rotten, and Simon will be a doting uncle.' She looked at Maeve. 'You say the baby's father is out of the picture. Do you think he'll try to find you when he gets out?'

'I don't think so. As I said before, a crazy, stupid, one-night stand with one of Simon's old friends, a hunk I've always fancied, but he didn't think to tell me he was going to prison. He hasn't answered one of my letters. Or Simon's attempts to talk to him. So that just makes me feel even more stupid.'

'Nope. Silly would be if you were waiting for him with open arms and no explanations.' Maeve made no move to go now they were finished and Tara glanced at her watch.

'If you want to come and help me with the young mums' class, it starts around one p.m. In the mothers' tearoom behind the desk.' Tara pointed.

'Thanks. I'll think about it. I might go for a walk now after sitting for so long.'

'Sure. Or have lunch and come back. I'll go home soon and grab a bite.' One of the midwives signalled to Tara as they walked out the door and Maeve shooed her towards the midwife.

'I'll go for a walk and come back.'

Tara arrived back at the manse half an hour later and Simon was in the kitchen, making coffee. He'd been waiting for them to return and, to him, it seemed like they'd been gone for hours. Maybe Maeve did have something wrong. Maybe his niggling worries did have some foundation. By the time Tara arrived, minus Maeve, he could barely contain his concern.

He forced himself not to pounce on her and gestured to the pot. 'You want one?'

'Love one, thanks. Black.'

'No sugar.'

'How did you know?'

He had to smile at that. He'd asked Louisa yesterday. 'So how did the antenatal visit go?'

'Fine.'

'So everything's fine?'

'I could tell you but then I'd have to kill you.'

'Come on. Reassure me.'

'Sure. We did bloods for thirty-six weeks and baby is moving well.' She rolled her eyes. 'Nothing else to tell until the blood results came back or we'd be speculating.'

'Speculating about what?'

'Nothing yet.' She was squirming and he wanted to know why, though it warred with his sense of fair play, but then there was big brother mode.

He saw the way Tara straightened her back and he felt a pang of guilt. She shouldn't have had to gird her loins against him.

She sized him up. 'You know, you're the one who said we should have a great rapport, and I'm just wondering how you think that will be built if I run to you with results and private information. I'm assuming you don't discuss your pregnant ladies with their relatives?'

He paused. Looked at her. 'No. You're right. I take that on board.' In fact, he was ashamed of himself for leaning on her but the niggling unease about his sister's health was also a concern. 'But if you're keeping something from me about my baby sister, I won't be happy.'

He couldn't seem to stop himself.

Tara was up for the challenge. 'Thanks for that. Didn't pick you for a bully. Silly me.'

True, and he didn't know what had come over him. Simon reached out, wanted to touch her briefly on her shoulder, but pulled back. 'Tara, I'm sorry. I have no right to harass you. Please accept my apology.'

Her phone rang and she glanced at the number. 'Now I know why you drive your sister mad. Good intentions and apologies. Would make anyone feel bad. But I'm not going there.'

She answered the phone. Listened and then said, 'Okay.'

She glanced at Simon with a bland smile. 'No problems. Gotta go.' Pulled open the fridge and grabbed an apple before she sailed out the door. 'See you later.'

Simon watched her walk away and he knew he'd been in the wrong—but she still hadn't given him answers.

The problem was that the last few days he'd been aware that something was not quite right about Maeve. He hated it had been a month since she'd last been seen, and he couldn't put his finger on the symptoms. But pressuring Tara was unlike him.

He guessed on Monday he'd be in a position to access his sister's blood pathology files when he went to work but he'd try not to look. It wasn't his practice to second-guess a colleague and he shouldn't start now. But it would be challenging not to peek.

CHAPTER SIX

MONDAY MORNING SAW Tara scooting around the ward, tidying up after their last discharged mother and baby. The first thing she'd done was check Maeve's results and thankfully they were totally normal so it was fine she hadn't mentioned anything to Simon.

As she worked she was thinking at least if Simon asked she could say everything was fine. Funny how she wasn't looking forward to the next time she saw him in one way and in the other she looked forward to just 'seeing him'.

Before she could think too much of it a car screeched to a stop out front and a harried-looking man she hadn't seen before leapt from the driver's side before Tara could open the passenger door.

'Her waters broke. She's pushing.'

Tara sent a reassuring nod towards the strained face of the woman seated awkwardly in the front seat, and wished this had happened earlier at handover so at least there would be two midwives there for the birth. Judging by the concentration that had settled over the woman's face and the tiny outward breaths she was making, that wasn't going to happen.

The man said, 'It's breech and they said Susan had to have a Caesarean birth in Brisbane.'

Tara doubted a Caesarean would be possible in the minutes they had left. 'Okay. I'll grab a wheelchair while you stand Susan up and we'll get inside at least.'

She was thinking breech, Simon, handy, and before she spun the strategically placed wheelchair out the door she pressed the little green button they used for paging help so that someone from the other side of the hospital could lend her a hand, even if it was only to phone the midwife and doctor on call.

'It's okay, Susan.' She spoke in a slow, calm voice, because people arriving at the last minute in labour wasn't that unusual, and she smiled again as she eased the woman into the chair and began pushing swiftly towards the door. 'You'll be fine. Help's coming, and we've had breech babies here before.' Not in her time but she'd heard the stories and Susan's belly didn't look full term so baby might be a little early as well. All good things for a breech delivery.

The stress on the husband's face eased a little and Tara shared additional comfort. 'The more worried Susan is, the more painful the contractions feel. That seems a shame so if everyone takes a deep breath and just accepts that baby is going to do this his or her way, we'll work it out.'

'Thank God, someone with sense.' The muttered comment from the woman who hadn't previously spoken startled Tara, and she had to bite her lip to stop a laugh, but then Susan was hit by another contraction and became far too busy to add further pithy comments.

The sound of footsteps meant help was almost here and by the time Tara had Susan standing up from the chair beside the bed Simon appeared at the doorway.

From worrying about when she saw him next to relief at his appearance. Another miracle. 'Simon. Great. This is Susan, who's just arrived. Waters have broken and she wants to push her breech baby out very soon.'

Susan glared at him and said, 'I'm not lying down to have this.'

'Sounds good.' Simon crossed the room quietly and shook the harried man's hand. 'Simon Campbell. Obstetrician.'

'Pete Wells, and my wife, Susan.'

Simon turned to Susan and touched her shoulder briefly while he glanced at her tight belly and then her face. 'Hi, Susan. First baby?' The woman nodded.

'And what date is your baby due?'

'Four weeks.'

'And breech, you think?'

'Was yesterday at ultrasound. We were on our way to Brisbane.'

'Unless you've noticed lots of movements since then, your baby probably still is breech.' He glanced at Tara. 'What's the plan?'

'The plan was a Caesarean in Brisbane, but Susan wants to stand up for a vaginal birth. So I thought that seeing you're here you could check and see where she's up to, and baby will tell us what to do. Unfortunately, Susan has to lie down for a part of that.'

Simon grinned at her. 'Interesting take. And I concur with it all.' He looked at Susan. 'You fine with those plans?'

'Perfect. As long as you are quick. I never wanted the Caesarean.'

'Ah,' said Simon, as Tara helped Susan un-dress and reluctantly lie down for the examination. 'A rebel.' Simon quickly but thoroughly palpated Susan's belly, stepped aside so Tara could also confirm the position of the baby, and then washed his hands and pulled on the sterile gloves. 'Baby taking after the mum? I'll be as quick as I can so you can stand up again.'

One minute later it was confirmed. 'Yep, breech. In perfect position. And ready to come.' He nodded at Tara. 'Best get another person here for baby and we can send them away if we don't need them.'

Tara crossed to the phone and called the switchboard then dragged a sheet-covered mat to the side of the bed in case Susan wanted to kneel down at some stage, and prepared her equipment. She'd never opened up sterile packs or drawn up needles so fast and excitement bubbled inside her. She was going to see her first breech birth.

Then Simon made it even more exciting. He spoke to the couple. 'I guess I should tell you that my specialty is promoting vaginal breech births at the Central Women's Hospital in Sydney, and if you don't mind I'd like to talk Tara through this birth so she can practise her own breech deliveries.'

He looked at Susan and then Pete. 'Is that all right with you?' Susan ignored Simon but nodded at Tara while she pushed, and Pete reluctantly agreed. Tara slid the little ultrasound Doppler over Susan's belly and they all heard the cloppety-clop of the baby's heartbeat. Susan's shoulders sagged with relief and she bore down with a long outward breath now she knew her baby was fine.

Simon went on. 'If baby decides to do anything tricky, I'll take over.'

Pete still didn't look happy but Tara was beginning to think poor Pete didn't handle stress well. 'We'll have to take your word for it,' he said.

'I guess that's all you can do.' Simon smiled

sympathetically as he pulled a chair across and sat down beside Tara, who was perched on a little wheeled stool, leaning towards Susan. 'Though I could give you my card and my phone to ring the Sydney ward but you might miss the birth.'

Because it was coming. A little pale crescent of buttock appeared as Susan breathed out and Tara felt the increase in her own heartbeat. OMG. She was going to cradle her first breech in a totally natural, peaceful environment and she didn't even have to feel terrified because Simon was right there beside her and she felt anything but.

'So Tara isn't going to touch the baby at all until the last moment. Your baby is nice and re-laxed at the moment and we don't want to scare it by putting a cold hand on him or her unex-pectedly. The heart rate is great and Tara will listen after every contraction to Susan's tummy.' Simon spoke in a very quiet conversational tone and Tara listened and obeyed every word without feeling like he was saying she didn't know what to do. It was obviously a skill he'd mastered.

Simon went on. 'Breech babies have the same mechanisms as head-first babies and once the hips are through it pretty well means everything is going to fit because the hips are roughly the same size as the shoulders.'

Tara hadn't realised that. Now they could see the little swollen scrotum and penis and Pete gasped and grinned when he realised what it was. Tara couldn't believe how fast everything was happening.

'You're doing beautifully, Susan,' she whispered. 'You're amazing. Not long now.'

'Okay.' Susan sounded strained but not frightened and Tara could feel the swell of emotion she felt at every birth at the miracles women could perform. It was all happening like clockwork. The pointy bottom seemed to be curving out sideways before it stopped and swivelled and Tara looked at Simon to ask if she should flick the leg out but he just smiled and shook his head.

The buttocks came down a little further and the foot lifted and sprang free. The other soon followed until baby was standing on tiptoe on the mat as his mother followed her instincts and crouched. Now the whole belly of the baby and the stretched umbilical cord could be seen.

'This is where we make sure the baby doesn't decided to spin the wrong way, but most of the time they drive better than we do.' Sure enough, the baby's body straightened, the stretched little chest lengthened, until there was just the top part of the baby inside.

'I can't stand it,' muttered Pete, as he twisted his fingers together, and Tara cast him a sympathetic look.

'I want to kneel,' Susan panted, and Tara cast a look at Simon.

'Just hang on for one sec, Susan. I'll move out of the way. You're almost there.' Tara pushed the chair away and knelt beside Susan as she turned sideways and with her reduced height the baby settled into a strange sitting position but with the movement the head slowly appeared, the little face flopped forward as the baby was born and Tara reached out and caught him before he fell forward onto his tummy.

'Well done,' Simon murmured with a definite thread of exultation in his voice. Tara felt a rush of emotion stinging her eyes as she dried the little body until the newborn screwed up his face and roared his displeasure.

She could see Simon's satisfaction in her management and she'd never felt so proud in her life. There was time for one brief glance of shared excitement and then it was back to the job.

'I'm just going to pop baby through your legs and you can see what you've had, Susan.' There was a flurry of limbs and cord and then Susan had her baby in her arms as she knelt upright. The face she turned to the three of them was exultant with fierce pride and joy. 'A boy. My vaginal breech birth boy. I knew I could do that.'

'Magnificently.' Simon shook his head with a twinkle in his eye that said he'd never grow tired of these moments, and Tara felt like she wouldn't want to sleep for a week she was on such a high.

Pete was in shock, and a little on the pale side as he flopped back into a chair Simon pushed up to him, while Susan was helped back up onto the bed by Tara. The new mum lay back with a satisfied smile and baby was just plain curious about the world and maybe even a little hungry.

They thanked the other doctor who had quietly arrived as unneeded back-up and he left. A few minutes later, after checking that all was well with Susan and the baby, Simon left too.

Tara leant against the doorpost, keeping watch that all was well now that she'd backed out of the circle of mother, father and child, and just soaked in the magic.

She couldn't believe it. Couldn't believe the experience that Simon had given her. Not just with his innate love of teaching and promoting breech birth to his less-experienced colleagues, but the ambience and peaceful joy of the occasion, because everyone, including her, had felt safe, and imbued with the faith that they'd had everything needed for the occasion. Her glorious moment! Because Simon had been there.

She'd never experienced anything like it. How could one man make that difference? It was a gift she hugged to herself.

Two hours later Susan was tucked up into bed for a well-earned rest but her eyes were wide and alert, baby Blake was tucked up in his little cot sound asleep beside his mother, and Pete snored gently in the big chair beside the window.

Susan and Tara looked at each other and smiled.

'I wish I could sleep,' Susan said dryly.

'It's the adrenalin from the birth,' Tara said quietly. 'Your instinct is to stay alert so you can snatch up your baby and run. You'll slowly calm down and drift off to sleep soon.'

'Thanks, Tara,' Susan said sincerely. 'From the first minute I saw you I knew everything was going to be fine.'

Tara had too. But Simon had ensured it really had gone well. He'd been amazing and she'd tell him so. 'I'm so glad. And thank you.' They grinned at each other as Tara gently shut the door to keep out the noises that might wake them.

CHAPTER SEVEN

SIMON DROPPED IN before the afternoon midwife arrived to see how Susan was faring.

'She's great. Talking about going home tomorrow. You going in to see her? Baby is awake and Pete's gone home.'

Tara was at the desk, completing Susan's patient notes. She went to stand and he put his hand up. 'Stay there. I'm just saying hello and I'll pop out to see you when I've finished.'

Tara nodded and carried on, wanting to have it all completed before the end of her shift. There was a mountain of paperwork when a baby was born, let alone when the woman arrived not expecting to have her baby with them, and she was transferring all the information they'd had faxed after the event from Brisbane.

But she still had to thank Simon and she didn't want him to leave without having the chance.

When Simon reappeared he had Blake with him. 'Susan's gone to the loo and Blake was complaining.' He carried the baby like a little football tucked onto his hip and his large hand cradling the baby's head with relaxed confidence. There was something incredibly attractive about a man comfortable with small babies and Tara hugged the picture to herself. Not that she was doing anything with it—just enjoying it.

Simon bounced the little baby bundle gently, feeling his weight. 'He's heavy.'

'Seven pounds on the dot.'

'Impressive for a breech.' He smiled at her. 'So were you.'

Tara could feel the heat in her cheeks. She hadn't been the amazing one. He'd instilled confidence in all of them, even the nervous Pete, so what was it about this guy that made her blush like a schoolgirl? Seeing that even when she'd been a schoolgirl she'd never blushed? 'I didn't do anything except put my hands out at the end, but I really appreciated the chance to be hands on, hands off. Thank you. And Susan was amazing.'

'It's okay, Tara. You were good because you didn't do anything. You did so well.'

'I can see why it's hands off now.' She changed the subject. Had never had been able to deal with compliments. Probably because she hadn't received that many in her life. She inclined her head towards Blake. 'You always been this good with babies?'

He grinned and she tried not to let the power of the smile affect her. Losing battle. 'I was a couple of years older than the eldest sister and Mum had three more pretty fast. So I guess I did get good with babies. I enjoyed helping with the girls and Mum was pretty busy by the time she had Maeve. I wasn't into dolls but it was always going to be obstetrics or paediatrics.'

He looked at Tara. Tried to see into her past. 'Were you a girly girl?'

Hadn't had the chance. 'What's a girly girl?'

'Dress-ups. A favourite doll?'

There had been a couple of shared toys she'd been allowed to play with but not her own. 'After my parents died I never owned a doll. So I guess not.'

His brows drew together but thankfully he changed the subject. 'What time do you finish?'

'Three-thirty.'

'Fancy another swim?'

Simon studied the strong features of the woman across from him. He became more intrigued the more he saw her. His four sisters had all been spoilt by everyone, including himself, and secure in their knowledge of their own attraction. Even Maeve in her current circumstances dressed and acted like the confident woman she was.

But Tara favoured the unisex look of jeans and T-shirts and now he knew that at work, despite the choices of the rest of the staff, she even favoured shapeless scrubs.

But in her plain black one-piece swimsuit she couldn't hide the fact she was all woman. A delightfully shapely woman with determination to the little chin and a wariness of being hurt that seemed to lurk at the back of her eyes.

An orphan. And a loner perhaps? 'Tell me about your childhood.'

'Why?'

'Because I'm interested.'

A wary glance and then she looked away. 'Nothing to tell.'

'Are you always this difficult when people want to get to know you?'

A clash of her eyes. 'Yes.'

'So did you always live in an orphanage or did you have foster-parents?'

'Both.'

He waited and she gave in with a sigh.

'I preferred the orphanage because at least I knew where I stood.'

He would have thought an orphanage would be way worse but he knew nothing. Hadn't ever thought about it. Didn't actually like to think about it when he looked at Tara. 'How so?'

'Being a foster-child is tricky. You know it's not permanent, so it's hard not to be defensive. If you let people get to you it hurts too much when you have to leave.'

He knew he should drop it, but he couldn't. 'Don't some foster-parents stay with the same children?'

Her face gave nothing away. 'I seemed to find the ones who shouldn't be foster-parents.'

He felt a shaft of sympathy for a little lost Tara. Found himself wanting to shake those careless foster-parents. It must have shown on his face.

'Don't even think about feeling sorry for me, Simon.' There was a fierceness in her eyes that made him blink.

And apologise. 'Sorry. I think my sisters had it too much the other way with people looking after them. I've always been protective. If you ask Maeve, too protective, and I guess I got worse when the truth came out that I really only had half the right.' It wasn't something he usually burdened others with twice but maybe unintentionally he'd trodden on Tara's past hurts and felt he should expose his own.

Of course Tara pounced on the chance to change the subject and he guessed he couldn't blame her. Served him right.

'So how old were you when you found out you had another father?'

The way she said it, like he had been lucky, if you looked at it from her point of view when she didn't even have even one father and he had two. Even privately complained about it. Novel idea when he'd been a cranky little victim despite telling himself to get over it.

He brought himself back to the present. 'After my dad's first heart attack, that would be the man I thought was my real dad, I heard my mother question whether I should be told about Angus. Not a great way to find out. Nineteen and I hadn't been given the choice to know my real dad for the whole of my childhood. And to be still treated like a child.' He hadn't taken it well and had half blamed Angus as well for not knowing of his existence.

'So how'd you find him? Angus?' Tara had looked past that to the interesting bit. Maybe he should have done that too a long time ago. She made him feel petty and he didn't like it.

'It was more than ten years ago, but at the time it all seemed to move too slowly. Took six months. He was on some discreet medical assignment overseas and the government wouldn't let me contact him. Then he came to see me and brought me here to meet my grandfather. It must have been a family trait because he hadn't seen his own dad for twenty years.'

'Louisa's husband?'

'Yep. Apparently Angus and Grandfather Ned fought over my dad's relationship with my mother, and when they ran away together and it didn't work out, he never came back here.'

She didn't offer sympathy. Just an observation as she glanced around. 'It's a very healing place.'

'Well, Angus brought me here to get to know him. And this was where he met Mia.'

He wondered if that was why he hadn't been able to commit to a relationship in the past. To fully trust people because even his own parents had betrayed him. He shook his head. Didn't know where all that angst had come from, it certainly wasn't something he'd talked about before, and if he'd stirred this kind of feeling in Tara by asking about her past, he could see why she didn't want to talk about it. When he thought about her life he felt incredibly selfish and self-indulgent complaining about his own.

She'd said Lyrebird Lake was a healing place. Maybe it was. Did that mean his coming here with Maeve meant it was his turn to move on? He mused, 'I don't know if it's the place or the people, but whenever I visit it seems when I leave here I'm usually less stressed.'

She laughed and he enjoyed the sound. 'Even if you lose some of your holidays to fill in for your dad and unexpected breech deliveries.'

'They're the good bits.' And he realised it was true. He smiled at her. 'The really good bits.'

'Like today.' She smiled back and the way it changed her face made him think of a previous conversation. Tara's glorious moment. She certainly looked the part.

He caught her fingers. 'Today has had some very magical moments.'

He smoothed the towel out of her grip and let it fall and gathered up her other hand. He half expected her to pull away but she seemed bemused more than annoyed. He tugged her closer until their hips met. Liking the feel of a wet Lycra mermaid against his chest, unconsciously he leaned in and her curves fitted his like they were designed for each other. He looked down at her long, thin fingers in his bigger hands, stroked her palm and felt a shiver go through her.

'What are you doing?' she whispered.

He had to smile. 'Enjoying another magical moment.'

Looked down into her face and then there was no way he could stop himself bending his head and brushing her lips with his. Watched her eyelids flutter closed and the idea that this prickly, independent woman trusted him enough to close her eyes and allow him closer filled him with delight.

Lips like strawberry velvet. A shiver of electricity he couldn't deny. 'Mmm. You taste nice.'

Her turn to smile as she opened her eyes and ducked her head to hide her face but he couldn't have that. Wouldn't have that as he slid one finger under chin, savoured the confusion in her eyes and face and then leant in for a proper kiss. She was like falling into a dream, soft in all the right places, especially her lips.

As she began to kiss him back there wasn't much thinking in his mind after that but a whole lot of feeling was going on. Until abruptly she ended it.

Tara felt as if she was floating and then suddenly realised she was kissing the man everyone loved. Who did she think she was? She pulled away and turned her back on him. Picked up the towel she'd dropped. Didn't know what had happened—one minute they'd been flirting and teasing, probably to get away from the previous conversations, and then he'd confused the heck out of her with the way he'd looked at her—and that kiss!

She could still feel the crush against his solid expanse of damp chest and was surprisingly still dazed by a kiss that had gone from gorgeously warm and yummy to scorching hot in a nanosecond.

And she'd thought he was a little stand-offish! This wasn't going anywhere, except a one-night stand, maybe if she was lucky a one-month stand. Well, she'd been as bad as him. She sighed and turned back to him with a smile that she'd practised over the years that shielded her from the world.

'Guess we'd better get back.'

He narrowed his eyes and there was a pause when she thought he was going to get all deep and personal or apologise, but he didn't. Thank goodness.

She just wanted to finish drying off and walk back to the manse. Maintain the reality that she was playing with a toy that didn't belong to her and if she kept touching it she'd be in deep trouble.

Simon really wanted to hold her hand, it would have been...nice? But Tara had tucked her fingers up under her elbows in a keep-off gesture that he couldn't help reading. Maybe he had come on a bit strong but, lordy, when he'd kissed her the second time the heat between them had nearly singed his eyebrows off. The thought made him smile. And grimace because it obviously hadn't affected her the way it had affected him. Did she realise the power those lips of hers held?

When they arrived back at the manse the kitchen was in chaos. Simon figured out that Louisa had cajoled Maeve into helping her assemble the Christmas tree and mounds of tinsel and baubles lay scattered across the kitchen table and cheesy Christmas tunes were playing in the background.

The manse had a big old lounge room but he knew every year Louisa put the Christmas tree up in the kitchen because that was the place everyone seemed to gravitate to—and this year was no different.

Simon loved the informality of it, unlike his mother's colour-co-ordinated precision, and he enjoyed the bemused expression, mixed with a little embarrassment left over from their kiss, on Tara's face as she looked round at him.

'Excellent timing, Simon,' Louisa said, as she handed him an armful of tiny star-shaped bulbs on a wire and a huge black plastic bag. She gestured vaguely to the screen door and he inclined his head to Tara and opened the door for her. The long post and rail veranda looked over the street and then the lake.

'Outside is where it really happens.' Good to have something to fill the silence between them. Awkward-R-Us. He waved the roll of bulbs at Tara and set about repairing the damage he'd done by kissing her.

'This is the start of the outside contingent. My job is to help Dad put these up when I'm home.' He pulled a little stepladder along behind him until he reached the end of the veranda and climbed up. Started to hang the tiny lights as far as he could reach before he climbed down again.

Tara was still looking bewildered and maybe still a little preoccupied from their kiss at the lake. He was sorry she was feeling uncomfortable, but he knew for a fact he wasn't sorry he'd kissed her. He wanted to do it again. Instead he carried on the conversation because she sure wasn't helping. 'These go along the top wooden rail. You can see them from down the street. Looks very festive.'

'I imagine it does.' She closed her eyes and he realised she was doing one of those breathing things he'd seen her do before and when she opened her eyes she was the old Tara again.

She smiled, so she must be okay, and he felt inordinately relieved. 'I'm not experienced at decorations. Put a few up in the ward last year when I worked Christmas week. Santa Claus was a big hit with the mums and their new babies.'

Now, there was a fantasy. Maybe he could dress up as Mr Claus and she'd sit on his knee. Naughty Simon. 'Santa has potential for lots of things.' He could feel the smile in his voice and packed that little make-believe away for later. Then he realised that, of course, she'd missed out on family Christmas for most of her life too. Not a nice thought. 'I'm guessing he didn't visit the home?'

She looked at him with disgust. 'Don't go there, Simon. I'm fine. They looked after me and I was never hungry. Lots of kids can't say that.'

Okay, he knew that, but there was more to being cared for than food in your belly, he thought as he hung each loop of Christmas lights over the tiny hooks under the eaves, and winced again at how easy his own childhood had been.

He glanced towards the kitchen, where his sister stood watching Louisa tweak the tree.

Maeve had been loved and cared for and told she was wonderful since the day she was born. A lot of the time by Simon because he'd thought the sun shone out of his youngest sibling. Though that wasn't doing him much good at the moment.

He remembered his father saying Tara was tough. He guessed she'd had to be. 'Okay. Moving on.' And he tried to. 'As you are inexperienced I will explain. You, Mrs Claus, have to hold the big ladder while I put the star up.'

'Louisa has a star?' The look she gave him

made up for everything. She appreciated him backing off. Okay. He'd avoid the orphanage topic but he still planned to make this Christmas special.

'Yep. In the bag.'

Tara undid the string and peered in. 'A blue one. Looks three feet tall?'

He was going down the stairs to the lawn. 'Goes on the corner of the roof.' He pulled out a large metal ladder from behind a water tank stand, and the long ladder reached all the way to the top of the roof.

Simon sneaked a look at her face, saw excitement growing as they put up the decorations, no matter how hard she tried to hide it.

She was loving this!

The thought made his heart feel warm and a feeling of delighted indulgence expanded in his gut. 'Louisa has everything Christmas. It started after she married Ned. Grandfather discovered she'd always wanted Christmas decorations and each year he bought something even more extravagant for her collection. She has a whole nativity scene with life-sized people for the front lawn, and all the animals move.'

'Now, that is seriously cool.' Tara's eyes shone as she looked at the ladder. Then she frowned as she looked back at him. 'If you can climb that and not worry, then parachuting would be a cinch.' She crossed over to him, carrying the star, and waited for him to put his foot on the bottom rung.

He looked at her but ignored the parachute comment. 'Hmm. The decorations are cool, but not when you have to assemble them and put them up, then pull them down every year. I could live without the ladder climb.' He grinned at her and knew she could tell he didn't mind. 'Dad usually does it but he asked me to start. Louisa likes it up before December and that's tomorrow.'

He sighed, glanced at the ladder and held out his hand. 'Better get it over and done with. At least there's clips up here for the star. It just snaps into a slot and the wiring is already in place. It will be exciting for the little girls when they come home.'

She grinned. 'You're a wonderful grandson. And brother.'

He edged up a step at a time. 'Don't think so. Sometimes I only see them once a year at Christmas.'

She raised her voice. 'They said you write to them.'

He stopped. Looked down at her. 'I send a pretty card or a funny postcard every now and then. They phone me on Sundays if I'm not working.'

She couldn't imagine what it would be like to have someone do that. Imagine if Simon did that for her? Her whole world would gain another dimension, and then she stopped herself. Smacked herself mentally. He was just a nice guy. A nice guy who seemed to like kissing her?

CHAPTER EIGHT

THE FOLLOWING SATURDAY was Tara's birthday. She hadn't mentioned it, so he hadn't, but he'd quietly arranged a cake at the place where they were going to breakfast after the jump.

He'd learnt something as a brother of four plus two sisters. Women loved surprises.

He didn't even know why he was looking forward to Tara's adventure when he hated the whole concept of risk, except now he wouldn't miss it because it involved Tara. He hoped he wasn't getting too caught up in the whole Tara fantasy. It wasn't like it was a date.

She'd started off quiet, and he'd wondered if she was sorry she'd asked him. In truth, the discussion had been before he'd kissed her, but then as they drew closer to the jump zone she became more animated.

He glanced across at her face, eyes shining, a huge grin on her face, and she squirmed in her seat like the kid she'd never had the chance to be. This was a whole new side to the woman he considered the most self-sufficient young woman he'd met, and he savoured her little bursts of conversation in a new way from his previous lady friends.

She had her own ideas, often contrary to his, on work, on politics, on sport even, but was always willing to listen to another point of view.

He'd rarely enjoyed a conversation so much. He could have driven all day with her beside him instead of doing what he'd come to do. Watch Tara jump out of a plane.

When they arrived Simon followed Tara from his car and almost had to run to keep up. Now, that was what he called eagerness to embrace the experience. He might even be starting to get her interest, even if he didn't share it.

He'd read the skydiving webpage when he hadn't been able to sleep last night. It had been intriguing with the way they mentioned 'changing your life with a jump', though he couldn't see how Tara's life needed changing in that way. She was the most centred person he knew to be around.

Apparently, sky-diving freed you of the minutiae of the everyday that could cloud the joys of living.

Okay, rave on, yet the expression had resonated with him and made him wonder with a startling moment of clarity if that was what he did.

He organised and pre-planned as much as he could, as if he could keep all the facets of his world—in his mind he could picture pregnant Maeve, so that included his sisters—in order and safe from the possibility of harm.

He glanced up as another plane droned over-head into a scatter of puffy clouds in the blue sky. Safe from harm? Well, that went out the window with sky-diving. Literally.

Simon shrugged and guessed he could imag-ine the small stuff didn't matter when you were hurtling at two hundred kilometres an hour through those clouds before your para-chute opened. If it opened. He shuddered and increased his pace.

Inside the flimsy building—how much money did they spend on this operation anyway, and just how safe were they?—Simon's gaze trav-elled around suspiciously until he realised what he was doing and pulled himself up. Tara would be saying he could draw bad luck with nega-tive thoughts, and despite his scepticism he re-focussed on the woman he'd brought here, and just looking at her made his mind settle.

She was grinning like there was no tomorrow.

He jerked his thoughts away from that one as she beckoned him over.

'Simon?'

Her expression puzzled him—eager, mischievous, with just a touch of wariness. 'They could squeeze you in if you wanted to change your mind.'

'And you're telling me this because?'

Her eyes glowed with excitement and for a minute there he wanted to take her outside this building and back her up against a tree and kiss the living daylights out of her. Then she said, 'Why don't you jump with me? Do it spontaneously.'

He blinked. One pleasant picture replaced with another he didn't fancy. 'Like spontaneous combustion. One whoosh and I'm gone?' She was dreaming. 'Then who would do all the things I do?'

Her voice lowered and she came closer until suddenly there seemed only two of them in the room. 'Stop thinking about everyone else for a minute. Do it for yourself. Be irresponsible for once and find out what it feels like. Change your life.'

There's nothing wrong with my life, he thought, but he didn't say it. Just stared into those emerald-green eyes that burned with the passion of a zealot. The woman was mad. 'Nope. But thank you. You go ahead and have your instructions for insanity and I will arrange breakfast for afterwards when you land on the beach.'

'They say it's the closest you'll ever get to flying on your own.'

'I read that.' He'd actually done a bit of almost-flying when he'd kissed a certain someone the other day. He was barely listening as he soaked in her features. How could he have ever thought this woman was average?

She looked at him for a moment and then

leant forward and kissed him quickly on the lips. 'Okay.'

Then she was gone, leaving an echo of her scent and the softness of her mouth that vibrated quietly in the back of his mind and all the way down to his toes. And a tiny insidious voice poked him with a thought. Imagine if it did change the way you lived. Not his work but his private life.

His lack of trust in relationships. The business of assembling scenarios so he could be sure he had all his bases covered. The worry about minutiae, like it said in the brochure. Possibly left over from the time he'd realised his own father had been totally unaware of him—when he should have checked if he had a son!

No way. He shut the thought down. Not today. But unconsciously, as he leant against the wall and watched her follow the instructions of Lawrence, her 'chute buddy' coach, he paid more attention as they prepared her for the way she left the aircraft and the way she had to bend her legs and point her toes as they landed.

He watched her tilt her head back, exposing her gorgeous tanned throat. Apparently that was so when you hurtled out of the plane your head didn't slam backwards and knock out the person who was going to pull the ripcord. Good choice. Tilt head. He could just imagine her. Wished he could see her do it. He grinned and looked away. No, he didn't. At least he was calmer than he'd thought he'd be, watching all this.

Simon glanced at the cost of the extravagant packages that could come with the jump and doubted she had enough for the whole experience to be filmed, captured in photographs as well and saved in a bound volume. He wandered discreetly over to the sales desk, enquired, and hoped like hell she wouldn't mind if he paid for the video/album package to arrive in the mail. He ensured Lawrence switched on his high-definition camera. It was the next best thing to being a fly on the wall without having to actually be there. And she'd have a permanent memento of the event.

She hopefully wouldn't take it up full time if she loved it. Simon found himself smiling as he drifted back to the doorway, where he leaned while he waited for her to finish her induction.

Then it was time for her to go. Go as in jump.

Tara bounced across the room with her harness all strapped between her legs and over her shoulders. Plastic wind protection goggles sat on top of her head and she radiated suppressed excitement like a beacon in a storm.

The two other people in her group seemed to radiate less exuberant anticipation. Right there with you, buddy, Simon thought with some amusement, and appreciated again that Tara did bring a sparkle into his day. As long as she didn't want him to join her he was quite happy to stand on the sidelines and enjoy the show.

* * *

Tara barely felt her feet on the floor. She couldn't wait for that moment when they tumbled out. She glanced back at her older instructor who carried the chute that would float them to the ground again and wanted to hug herself with excitement. Or have Simon hug her.

She glanced at Simon, who watched her with a whimsical expression on his face. It was so cool he'd come with her. Even if he didn't want to jump, and it had been a pretty big spur-of-the-moment ask, he still looked fairly happy. She'd been a little afraid of that. That he'd radiate stress vibes and doomsday foreboding but he'd surprised her with how calmly he was taking it and how supportive he was.

She had an epiphany that maybe real men didn't have to do crazy things to be in tune with her. Look at her last man. He'd been crazy and had turned out to be a loser of the highest order so maybe the opposite worked.

She knew for a fact that Simon was far from a loser but she also knew she wasn't looking long term for someone like him. People like him spent their lives with prim and proper doctors' wives, not someone who wanted to seek thrills and drift from town to town like her. People like Simon hadn't been brought up in orphanages and foster-homes.

But you could kiss those people. The ones you weren't going to marry. It was a shame she'd enjoyed it so much because the idea of kissing Simon again intruded at the wrong times—like that mad moment when she'd asked him to jump and then kissed him.

But she wasn't worrying about that now and peered ahead to the tarmac where their little plane waited patiently for them. Excitement welled in her throat as they all paused at the gate and the actual jumpers farewelled their ground crew.

'Good luck. You look beautiful.' Simon's

words took her by surprise and she could feel the smile as it surged from somewhere in her over-excited belly.

'Thank you. So do you.' She grinned at him and he leaned in and kissed her firmly on the lips so that she knew she'd been kissed. For the first time the ground felt a little firmer under her feet and the haze she'd been floating in sharpened to reality. Luckily, that made it even more exciting.

The next fifteen minutes was spent crammed into the plane as they climbed in a slow spiral up to fifteen thousand feet. She sat perched on the lap of her chute buddy and surprisingly time seemed to pass very quickly with the hills towards Lyrebird Lake in the distance and the white sand of the beach underneath them.

They were going to land on the beach below the lighthouse and apparently Simon would already be there with the ground crew waiting for them to land.

Her chute buddy was fun and kept saying how relaxed she looked. But this wasn't something she was afraid of.

Finally they reached fifteen thousand feet, the roller door slid back along the roof and the cold wind rushed in.

He'd told her it was one degree outside but it would only take thirty seconds to get back to warm air, but she doubted she'd have time to feel temperatures as they hurtled through the clouds.

The boy next to her, now securely strapped to his chute buddy, cast an imploring look at the safety of the plane and then, with one wild-eyed glance at the occupants, disappeared.

'Let's go, Tara,' Lawrence shouted in her ear, and he edged his bottom and Tara as well, balanced on his lap, towards the opening and swung both their legs out until their backs were to the plane. Below them the ocean and the beach curved below under the scattered clouds.

She pushed her head back into Lawrence's shoulder and then they were out. Wind rushed past their faces, she had a brief glimpse of the plane above them in the sky and then they were facing the ground with the wind rushing into her face and her hands clenched tightly on the chest straps.

Funnily, even in that moment, she could see Simon's face. She grinned at the image and stared out into the vacant air in front of her. 'Woo-hoo.'

Simon had watched the plane disappear into the clouds.

Fifteen minutes later he watched the blue parachute as it came into view, imagined the grin on her face, the joy in her eyes and found himself very keen to see her feet touch the ground. Though no doubt she'd be wanting the descent to last for ever.

At the last minute he pulled his phone from

his pocket and videoed her landing. She waved as she sailed past, and he chuckled out loud. This had been fun and he'd been dreading it.

She landed smoothly on her bottom with her feet out in front of her, strapped like a little limpet to her chute buddy, and with a couple of snaps of the buckles she was free to stand and twirl around with excitement. He grinned as he watched her.

Later when he took her to the little restaurant on the river for a late breakfast she couldn't stop talking, reliving the experience, and he watched her shining eyes blink and frown and widen as she told the tale of her tumble from the aircraft, the whoosh of the parachute opening and the moment when she'd seen him watching her land.

Then he watched her eyes widen wistfully when a birthday cake was carried across the room and she glanced behind them to see where it was going. But his breath caught in his throat when he saw her eyes fill with tears when she realised it was hers. What was wrong? Had he done wrong?

He'd upset her and he didn't know why. 'It's yours. For you. Happy birthday, Tara.'

She just sat there staring at the lit candles as they burnt merrily. The candles started melting and began to dribble wax down onto the cake. Spluttered and dripped. Still she didn't blow them out.

'Blow them out.'

She looked at him. Her eyes still looked haunted. Then she whispered, 'Are you sure?'

'Quick.'

The waitress and chef who had followed the cake out were looking at each other, not sure what was going on, as they waited to sing like they did every time a cake was ordered.

Then she blinked, shook her head and blew them out. Almost defiantly. Certainly with ample power. To her horror, she even blew wax onto the tablecloth. Blushed and glanced at the waitress and her 'Sorry' was drowned out by the lusty singing of 'Happy Birthday'. Then she did cry.

The waitress and the chef bolted back to the kitchen and Simon handed her a napkin. Tara hid her face in it.

'Don't ever do that to me again.'

With startling clarity he suspected what was wrong. 'Have you ever blown candles out on a cake before, Tara?'

She glared at him. 'Not since I was six. As if you couldn't tell.'

'No cakes at the orphanage?'

'A hundred children would be a cake every three days. I didn't even know it was my birthday half the time. You couldn't know—I understand that—but it's never been a big day for me.'

He didn't want to think about a hundred kids without birthdays because it hurt all the way down to his toes. 'So why the parachute jump this year?'

She shrugged. 'Coincidence and maybe Lyrebird Lake warmth. They had a birthday party for Louisa and it was very cool. Started me thinking about a new life and a celebration that I had control of and wasn't using.'

'So a present?'

'Yep. That's my present to myself. I can't really afford it but…' she shook off the melancholy and gave him a watery smile '…it was so worth it.' She straightened her shoulders. Smiled at him again, though still a little misty-eyed. 'Thanks for the cake, Simon, and sorry for the drama. It just took me by surprise. I blew some candles out once and they weren't mine. Got in all sorts of trouble so just had a bit of a time slip there.'

'Well that cake was a hundred per cent yours and even the singing was good.'

She glanced towards the kitchen with a little

embarrassment still on her face. 'Very good. They must think I'm mad.'

'I'm sure they're thinking you must have a very good reason for acting as you did. Or they think I upset you.'

Her first cake with candles? Damn it, he wished he could turn up on her birthday and buy her a cake every year until she was so blasé about it she didn't notice. Then he listened to the wild thoughts in his head. How had he got to this point?

Because seeing Tara every year for the rest of his life didn't seem an unreasonable thing. But that was crazy.

After breakfast they went back to check out the beach. Simon kept saying she'd eaten and she wasn't allowed to swim for an hour but, seriously, she only wanted to splash in the waves anyway.

They stripped down to swimsuits and she kicked a skid of water his way.

After some serious splashing in his direction Simon stopped watching her with a smile on his face and started to chase her. She was pretty fast.

But he was faster. When he caught her and lifted her, spun her, held against his strong broad chest like a prize, it was as exciting as falling through the air this morning.

She'd always watched others do this, dreamt of doing it herself one day with some hero, and now here she was, with this gorgeous guy tossing her around like she was a lightweight as he shuffled on the sand and pretended to throw her into the water. She squeaked in mock terror, feeling like she was in a movie, a fabulous romantic movie, and while she knew it was just that, a fantasy that would stop when the hour or two was up, she was darned well going to enjoy every fabulous second of it.

Plus it was her birthday. She was the birthday

girl and Simon would not let her forget it. That was very cool.

Then Simon walked purposefully forward through the knee-high waves until he sank into the surf with her still in his arms and the cold salt water foamed around them. She could feel the core of warmth where their skins still connected and she couldn't do anything except turn her face to him and lean in for a kiss. A salty, exuberant kiss that was her way of saying thank you.

He must have been waiting because his arms tightened even more firmly around her and the kiss spiralled into a hot, hungry, searing feast of strength and softness and sliding tongues that were as hot as the water was cold around them. She grabbed on tighter and jammed her breasts harder against his chest and they didn't come up for air until a bigger than normal wave smacked them in the head and they broke apart coughing and spluttering and finally laughing.

Phew. She'd needed that bucket of reality because she'd been getting swept away in the fantasy of it all.

She swam away from him, bobbed with the waves, their feet still touching the golden sand below their toes but rising up and down with the cool green waves as her heart rate slowly began to settle.

This had to be the best birthday ever.

CHAPTER NINE

BACK AT THE manse life carried on as usual. Maeve slowed down even more as her baby grew and weighed her down, but her nausea had eased, although her mood remained sombre. Tara suspected she held unrequited affection for the baby's father and wondered if maybe someone should try again to contact him by phone. But that was for Maeve and she had enough happening.

Last night another of Tara's caseload women had had her baby and Tara had been up most of the night, but when she'd woken after lunch she'd felt strangely unsettled so she'd come out to the manger on the front lawn to find her peace.

Everything was so...Christmassy. She felt like

a minor character who'd forgotten her lines. Presents were appearing under the tree inside and she'd started to buy little gifts for everyone but lacked the experience to know how much to spend so had gone for quirky.

With combined family enthusiasm Louisa had managed to assemble her Christmas nativity scene on the front lawn. Tara had been surprised that the little straw-filled crib was empty despite the adoring looks and nods from the mechanical Mary, Joseph and the three wise men, until Simon had whispered that baby Jesus would arrive on Christmas morning.

There was something very centred about the anticipation of the baby that appealed to Tara. When she needed to get away to think she ended up on the garden seat that had a clear view of the people and animals in front of the manger. The whole concept of sharing their front lawn with the town took a bit of getting used to so she tried to come when it was deserted.

Those crazy manger animals nodded twenty-four seven and at night floodlights bathed the area.

During the day it wasn't unusual for children to drop by on the way home from school to check out the display and in the evenings families wandered down and oohed and ahhed and discussed what was new this year.

Angus and Mia had brought back an outdoor train set that ran on solar lights, and it chugged around the lighted Christmas tree on the lawn with pretend presents in the carriages behind. That one was a big hit with the little boys. Tara was secretly very impressed with it too.

Then she noticed Simon coming towards her with a determined stride and her pulse rate jumped at the grin he was sending her way. She'd been busy with her caseload women and hadn't seen him for more than a few minutes in the last few days since the parachute jump and beach. It was probably for the best because she was taking heed of her sensible side.

'There's a parcel for you, Tara.' He handed her a thick, flat package and she took it and turned it over in her hands but really she was absorbing the vibration between them as Simon sat down. There was a little gap between their bodies and the air seemed to be vibrating in the space. Very unsettling. He nudged her.

'Go on. Open it.'

Something was going on because there was definite mischief in his eyes as he waited for her to open the parcel.

She glanced down at the address. 'It's from the parachuting club.'

'Let me guess. You've become a life member.'

She had to laugh at that. 'Only if they want a resident midwife—but I don't imagine there's a lot of call for parachuting pregnant ladies.'

'Perhaps not.' He was still waiting for her to open it obviously.

'Aren't you going to leave me in peace?' She looked across and raised her eyes. 'Sticky beak?'

'Yep.'

She smiled and began to ease open the package, careful not to tear any of the envelope.

He huffed out his impatience. But he was pretending. 'Rip it!'

'No.' Shook her head. 'Envelopes can be reused. And it's not like I get many parcels.'

He folded his arms and she could feel his eagerness. She began to suspect what it was. Oh, my. 'Did you buy me the package, Simon?'

She surprised a look of wariness on his face she hadn't expected. He didn't say anything, just waited for her to pull it out.

When she did she couldn't speak. It was a bound volume of at least a hundred photos from right at the beginning of her instruction session to the moment she actually launched into space and all the way down until they landed. And then she saw the DVD.

She'd seen the camera on Lawrence's arm but had assumed it was there for safety reasons and had been sort of aware they'd been filming some of the jump. Not the whole lot!

If she thought about it she'd guessed some people might change their mind and buy packages after the jump. She'd lusted after one but had decided it was an expense she hadn't needed.

And Simon had bought her the full extravaganza. How did she thank him for something so huge—it was too huge—but it wasn't the sort of gift you could give back and say, *You keep it*. He just kept taking her breath away.

His voice was worried when she didn't say anything. 'Hope that's okay? I know how independent you are. But I just thought everyone would like to see your adventure too—without having to jump,' he added hastily. 'I can afford it, you know.'

'I guess you can. And it was a lovely thing

to do. Probably the loveliest thing anyone has done for me—except maybe the birthday cake the other day.' She leaned across and kissed his cheek but it was a dutiful kiss. 'But that's it. Don't start buying presents for me, Simon. I move a lot and can't build up possessions.' Or unreal expectations.

He shook his head. 'You don't *have* to move a lot.'

He just didn't get it. The world always moved you on when you started to love a place. 'Sure. Okay. And thank you.'

She could feel the tears pushing one way as she pushed them back the other but more than that she wanted to look at the pictures and re-immerse herself in the jump so she could forget the look in his eyes. The more she thought about it and the reason Simon had said he'd done it, the more touched she was.

She was an ungrateful wretch with no gift-receiving skills. Where the heck did you get those skills? She leant across and kissed him on the mouth this time. The anticipation was building. 'I'm sorry. Thank you. It is great.' She glanced at him under her brows. 'Wanna look with me?'

He seemed to deflate with relief and she realised he wasn't as calm as he looked. Maybe Simon was having a hard time dealing with the undercurrents between them too? An intriguing thought that could come back to haunt her.

He slid next to her until their thighs were touching, and she wondered what the passing manger lovers would think about Dr Campbell snuggling up to the midwife, but then she gave up and prepared to open the book. The relief in his face confirmed her suspicion. He'd been worried he'd upset her and she guessed she could get tetchy so he'd been brave to push ahead and buy it. The guy was certainly a keeper. Such a darned shame she couldn't.

Instead, she opened the album and the first picture captured the day. There she was, the plane disappearing above them, and an expression of sheer exhilaration on her face as they freefell into the clouds. She looked at Simon and there was a look of indulgence on his face that made her pause and then dismiss the ridiculous idea that he might care for her just a little more than she'd thought.

After a hilarious fifteen minutes sitting on the bench, poring over the album, they took the DVD into the house, where they dragged Louisa and Maeve into the lounge room to watch it on the old television.

During the ten-minute DVD Louisa gasped and covered her mouth and even Maeve laughed out loud and expressed her envy that Tara had done something she'd wanted to do. Then it was over and Louisa and Maeve went back to the kitchen and she had to go and check on one of her early labour mums.

'Thanks again, Simon.' She'd probably kissed him enough, she admitted with a definite tug of despondency as she turned away. 'I'd better get going on my home visit.'

Simon nodded and held the door for her and he didn't lean down enough for her to attempt any sort of cheek-kissing salutation like he did. But he did say, 'So when are you going to take me on your bike?'

That stopped her. She'd thought it unlikely this conversation would ever come up. And it wasn't like she could say no now. In fact, she owed him big time. 'Any time you're ready.'

He shrugged. 'I'm officially off call and ready when you are. Make a date and do your worst.'

She looked him over coolly but inside she was doing a little shaking and wondering if this would be a clever thing to do. Simon, pressed up against her, his arms holding on tight. Leaning into corners together. His strong thighs alongside her thighs. But there was barely a wobble in her voice when she answered, thank goodness. 'I don't have a worst. Where did you want to go?'

He shrugged. 'It doesn't really matter as long as I get to try the full experience.'

This was getting weirder. Whatever that meant. 'Fine. Then Saturday. We'll go up to the lookout, it's a nice drive through the forest and it's a great place to watch the sunset.'

'You're on.'

Almost enthusiastic. Her voice held a hint of indulgence. 'You'll be wanting to parachute next.'

'I haven't ruled it out in the far distant future.'

She looked at him and he was smiling but whether he was teasing or serious she couldn't work out. What she could read made her cheeks feel hot. She almost wished he didn't look at her like that because it was going to be incredibly hard some time in the definite future when the feeling it gave her was lost.

But then her sensible side, the one that said

she would survive no matter what, decided that being with Simon was like parachuting—the rush was incredible but the reality was the ground waiting for you. But it didn't mean you shouldn't enjoy the ride. This would never last but it was wonderful while it did and from now on she was going to take what was on offer with open arms.

On Saturday Simon was waiting for her when she returned from an unscheduled home visit. One of her caseload ladies was having breast-feeding problems so Tara had sat with her for the last feed until mum and baby were back in sync.

She glanced at her watch. 'Do we still have time before sunset? Or do you want to wait until tomorrow afternoon?'

'I've been waiting all day to hang off the back of your bike.' The words were jaunty but the unease was not quite hidden on Simon's face and belied his statement as he picked up his backpack.

She had to smile at that. 'Liar.' She watched him slide his arms into the shoulder straps and hoist the pack onto his back in one adroitly muscular movement. Dragged her eyes away. 'What's in the bag?'

'Never you mind. You worry about me and I'll worry about the bag.'

Oh, she was worried about him all right. 'Sounds intriguing. You'll have to wait while I change.' She glanced at his long jeans and solid shoes and nodded approval. 'I don't ride in shorts either.'

'Tell me you come in leather.' A wicked wink suggested he was fantasising and hoping she'd come to the party.

'I can do.' She raised her brows suggestively, playing along with him, and couldn't believe how much fun this stuff was. 'But normally only for long trips.' She tossed over her shoulder, 'You'll just have to wait and see.'

Simon watched her scoot along the hallway and despite his misgivings about actually being a pillion passenger on a motorbike he had the feeling Tara would be worth waiting for. Ten agonising minutes later he wasn't disappointed. Sweet mother!

Tara's long sexy legs were encased in skin-tight, dull black leather trousers and high black boots. The material's softness curved around the cutest tight little butt, and his fingers curled in his pockets. Untucked, she wore a white shirt with a plunging neckline and a short, black, sleeveless leather vest was loosely laced over the top. Yep, that completed the outfit, and he had to jam his hands into his pockets. Now he really couldn't wait to get on her bike.

She looked like something out of a Hell's Angels fantasy world and he was glad they were going into the country and not on the main road.

He was man enough to prefer to have her to himself like this and couldn't wait to have the excuse to hold her around her waist and snuggle up against her. Must have a latent dominatrix fantasy he hadn't known about and he grinned to himself as he followed her outside and around to the carport.

She pulled the cover off the bike and sat astride as she wiggled it backwards. No, she wouldn't let him help pull it out and face it the right way, so he did the next best thing and just stood there and enjoyed the show. He decided that Tara was a strong little thing, and the thought made him even hotter, in a non-weather-related way.

Tara set about checking everything was right and finally gave him the nod. She handed him her helmet and pulled her spare on.

'So have you ever been on a bike before?'

'No.'

'Okay. So hold on loosely around my waist,

tighter on the corners. Sit up straight. Try and lean gently into the corners in the same direction as I do. If you find the corners too hard just don't lean the opposite way.'

'Yes, ma'am.'

'Good. Remember that. I'm the captain.'

The captain. He kept his tongue firmly between his teeth when he really wanted to say, *Aye, Aye*, and grin at her. Or kiss her. Definitely the last. He'd been waiting all day for this moment, the sliding on behind her thing, of course, not the actual motorbike thing, and as he climbed on and shifted in until his thighs were up against her leather-clad buttocks it was as exciting as he'd imagined. See. He could be adventurous.

Initially she took off slowly and rode along the back streets of the lake and Simon found that holding onto Tara while the big bike vibrated strongly beneath them was a very pleasant experience. He'd decided that worrying about accidents wouldn't help at all so tried conscientiously to focus on the other, more positive things.

Lots of delightful sensory input to distract him, especially the really tactile stuff, like Tara's waist was the perfect width beneath his hands, and he tried not to dwell on the fact if he reached up and spread his fingers he could span her rib cage and even brush the undersides of her breasts. Felt the uncomfortable tightness in his jeans and dragged his mind away from that scenario because it was just too uncomfortable.

Her buttocks pressed against him as they sped up an incline and if he tightened his arms his chest could stretch forward and lean into her back any time he chose.

'You okay?' She turned her head a little and he heard the words. She sounded strained but it was probably the wind snatching them away.

'Fine,' he shouted back. Conversation was impossible and he didn't even try. They'd picked up speed and were climbing a narrow tarred road that curved around the mountain towards the lookout. Heavy forest growth hid the thousands of cicadas that were humming as a quiet thrum under the rumble of the engine as they rode along, and every now and then a circling eagle would soar into view.

The wind rushed past and he enjoyed the sensation of the breeze along his arms. Even got some of the reasons Tara enjoyed the freedom of riding her bike so much.

They came to a long curve in the road and he'd learnt to lean the same way as she did and felt a little of the thrill of adrenalin she'd talked about. He could imagine it would be even better if he was the one steering and Tara was holding on—maybe something for the future to consider.

By the time they arrived Simon was so comfortable behind Tara he'd moved on to enjoying the view but couldn't help appreciate how comfortable and secure he felt in such a short time—testament to her skill and confidence. It still made him shake his head how she had so much control over the powerful bike considering it was bigger than she was for a start and had a whole lot more horsepower than she did.

He got off first and she propped it sideways on its stand. Flipped her helmet open to talk as she fiddled with the chin strap. 'Enjoy that?'

'Yes, thank you. I actually did. And I'm very impressed with your riding skill.' His helmet was off and he stepped forward to assist her. She let him, just—irritable little thing. She obviously didn't like asking for aid so it was nice she was learning to take some help from him.

The strap came undone and she lifted her helmet off. 'I gave you the easy one to undo.'

'Ah,' he teased. 'Of course. Thank you.' He looked around. They had the lookout to themselves. 'I came up here years ago but had forgotten how amazing the view is.'

They walked towards the grassy edge that disappeared into the valley below. There was a little secondary platform screened from the road and he jumped down to the next level and held out his hand. 'It's even nicer down here.' He couldn't help the satisfaction in his voice. This was an excellent place.

Hmm, Tara thought. Simon looked pretty darned hot down there. More than hot. And there was a little bit of heat singing her even up here.

A tall, tanned, smiling hunk of a man, one she admired privately and professionally, holding his hand out to invite her to join him. Though, having been sandwiched against him for the last thirty minutes, she wasn't sure that jumping into his arms would be safe at this minute.

Looked a bit of a set-up, Tara admitted with an inward jiggle of awareness, and couldn't help but remember what had happened after the lake, and definitely after the beach frolic, but she had way more clothes on this time. Note to self. Keep clothes on.

She shrugged mentally and took his hand as she landed beside him. Sucked in the fresh, cooler air and shaded her eyes to estimate how much longer they had to get back before dark.

'Probably two hours till sunset?' In the distance the lake sparkled in the afternoon sun, and the mountains behind which the sun would sink were already dusted with gold. Simon was also dusted with gold, everything felt golden, and she could feel the prickle of nervousness again. 'I like this road for a run on the bike. I've been here a few times.'

The air shimmered between them with a bigger thrum than three million cicadas and the awareness in the pit of her stomach growled like a nasty case of hunger pains. Maybe it *was* hunger pains. She glanced at his backpack as

Simon put it down on the grass. 'So? What's in the backpack?'

'A picnic for the princess, of course. Louisa is renowned for her picnic hampers. And I'm not without a few surprises.'

Surprises. Yep, he liked surprises. The first time, with the birthday cake, she'd cried. She was not going to cry this time. 'Ooh. Picnic. Cool.'

'Prepare to be amazed.' He crouched down. Withdrew the tartan rug and spread it in the centre of the grassed area so they were facing the view. He patted the rug beside him. 'Come on. Down you come.' He undid the laces on his shoes and pulled them and his socks off.

She was distracted for a minute. He had very attractive feet. Long toes and very masculine-looking feet. He wiggled the toes and she caught his eye. He was grinning at her.

Maybe she could lose her own boots? She sat down, feeling a little heated, a little confined in her outfit, and before she realised what she was doing she'd removed her vest and was reaching down for her boots.

Simon was pretending not to look as he studied the hamper with only occasional sideways glances at her cleavage. Ogler. She laughed at herself. No use getting prudish about that. Why had she worn that shirt if she hadn't wanted him to appreciate? And she guessed she would have been miffed if he'd sat there and stared at the view and not her.

'Yep, that's more comfortable.' She stretched out her legs and leaned back, resting her weight on her hands.

'Non-alcoholic sparkling wine?' Simon held out a plastic champagne flute and Tara grinned.

'Classy.'

'Story of my life.'

'Not mine.'

'Some people are classy no matter what. You're one of them.'

Aw, he said the nicest things, and she could feel the prickle in her throat. Not crying. Ha, said a little voice, you said you weren't taking any of your clothes off either.

He leant over and dull-clunked their plastic flutes in a toast. 'To the classiest lady I know.'

'To the smoothest man around.' She took a sip and it wasn't bad for a soft drink.

He took a sip and then put his flute down on the lid from the container that held cheese, nuts, celery and carrot sticks, and in the middle was a big dollop of guacamole.

'You had that in the backpack?'

'I told you Louisa was the picnic queen. She has a whole set of bowls she uses for hampers.' He pulled out another that held marinated chicken wings.

By the time they'd picked and sighed over the food, laughed at how strangely hungry they were, and had eaten far too much whenever the conversation flagged, the sun hovered over the distant mountains like a gold penny about to drop.

Simon had packed the food back into the insulated backpack, Tara was gazing into the small pool of liquid in her glass, and the playful mood had deepened back into the awareness that had always been there but which now eddied between them like the afternoon breeze.

'It's been fun, Simon.'

'It has, Tara.' There was a tinge of amusement in his voice as he slid across next to her. When his hip touched hers he lay back on the rug, one hand behind his head and the other he used to catch her hand.

'Those clouds over there look like a castle with a dragon.'

She looked up, squinted and frowned. 'Where?'

'You'll have to lie down to see.'

'Ha.' But she lay down and he pointed and she could just see what he meant before the turbulence slowly rearranged the puffy paintwork in the sky into something else.

'I can see a dinosaur.'

'Where?'

'To the left of the dragon.' She lifted her hand and he followed where she pointed.

'That's not a dinosaur. More of an elephant.'

She giggled. 'That's not an elephant.'

He rolled onto his side and she could feel him watching her. So this is was what they meant when they said 'basking'. Tara felt herself 'basking' in Simon's appreciation and it was a feeling she'd never really experienced. Could certainly grow accustomed to it too if she had the un-likely chance of that.

He leant over and kissed the tip of her nose. It was unexpected and she sneezed.

Simon flopped back and laughed out loud. 'It's hard being a man, you know,' he complained. 'I have to make all the moves and then she sneezes.' He put his hand over his eyes. 'I had this fantasy that this incredibly sexy woman— dressed in black leather, mind you—would attack me and have her wicked way with me, or at least kiss me senseless.' He sighed again. 'But it hasn't happened.'

Tara rolled over to face him, with her arm tucked under her cheek. Then, with a 'nothing dared, nothing gained thought behind her eyes', she climbed on top of him until she had one leg on either side of his body and her weight resting on her hands. She leant in and kissed his lips, once—he tasted so good—twice—*mmm... yum*—and a slower third time that threatened to turn into something bigger until she sat up. Feeling pretty impressed with her own daring, actually. 'Consider yourself attacked.'

'Mmm.' His eyes had changed to sleepy sexy and his hands reached up and slowly pulled her face down to his. 'I could get used to this.'

The sun was setting. And she wanted nothing more than to lose herself with Simon in this private place above the world. But she wasn't quite sure this was the right time—goodness knew where that thought had come from. 'I think it wouldn't be as much fun in the dark.'

He smiled lazily and kissed her neck. 'You sure?'

'Mmm. Maybe it would be.' She had no doubt it would be. No, Tara. Stop it, the voice of reason nagged in her ear. 'But I don't make out on deserted roads with bikers.' She said it as a joke to lighten the moment, because Simon had been on his first bike ride now.

He pretended to be disappointed. He kissed her again. 'I should have known that about you.' He hadn't given up hope.

But then she thought of Mick. The picture of a dishevelled biker. And she guessed she had. But she'd never really seen that until the end. She'd seen the lost little boy from the orphanage. The brother of her best little friend who had died so tragically young and someone who had needed her. She shuddered to think what Simon would have thought of Mick.

Simon's face changed and obviously, unless he could read her mind, he thought it was something else. 'You okay? I didn't mean to upset you. Hell, Tara, I think you're amazing. You blow me away and yet you make me feel so amazingly good.'

He rolled her off him and sat up. Reached down and pulled her up to sit next to him, tucking her into his side with his arm around her shoulders. 'Not sure how you do that but it's a great feeling. There's no pressure for anything else.'

'Ditto.' This guy was too much. Too nice, too amazing—for her. He'd be gone in a couple of weeks and she'd look back and wish she had made love with him. It was a gift to be here with him, right at this moment, and she was throwing it back because she was too scared of the moment—or was she too scared of the emptiness later?

Simon was like the foster-home she knew she'd have to leave. It really was better not to suffer the separation. But it felt so good to be tucked into his side, his strong arm around her shoulder. Close to him.

'You could still hold me, Simon.'

He cuddled her into him, gave the impression he couldn't get close enough, then lifted her onto his lap. 'Can't think of anything I'd rather do.'

So they sat there. Tara was still on Simon's lap as the sun set with a magnificent orange glow that turned to pink and purple in front of their eyes, reflecting off the lake, and she snuggled into his shoulder as peace seeped into her.

Then she heard the strangest thing. It sounded almost like her motorbike but distant. The throbbing roar of her Harley-Davidson. For a horrible moment she thought Mick had found her then remembered she had the bike.

Simon shifted her off his lap and stood up as she scrambled to her feet herself.

But when they looked her bike was there. Less than ten feet away from them and definitely still and quiet. Then the noise came again. The louder roar of the engine then the sound of a bike idling. It came from the bushes across the car park and Simon started to laugh.

'What was that?'

'If I'm not mistaken, that, dear Tara, was our lyrebird.'

'You're kidding me. How could a bird make that noise?'

'World's greatest mimickers. They can sound like babies, chainsaws...' he grinned '...and apparently Harley-Davidson motorbikes.' Simon slipped his hand into hers and pulled her into his embrace. Kissed her gently. 'I'll have to apologise to my dad. Lyrebirds make amazing noises. That's pretty special.'

Still distracted, she kissed him back but not with her full attention. 'Not possible.'

But the sound came again and closer to them. To the side there was a rustle of bushes, the crack of tiny twigs, and she twisted her head to see past Simon's shoulder and then she saw it. A small grey-brown bird the size of a chicken, his reddish-brown throat lifted as he gazed at her. But it was the two long feathers that hung each side of his tail that told her what it was.

She whispered. 'Simon. Turn slowly and look to your left.'

Simon turned his head and saw it. A slow smile curved his mouth. 'I told you!' He squeezed her. 'Our lyrebird.'

He'd said 'our' again. She hugged that defiantly to herself and ignored her voice of caution. 'Why doesn't it run away?'

He grinned cheekily. 'Well, it knows I don't

want to move.' He squeezed her gently. Looked down into her face. 'I really don't want to.'

But the lyrebird could. He strutted across to a little mound of dirt about six feet from them and climbed to the top, where he spread his gorgeous tail. Swivelled his head to glance at them as if to tell them to pay attention, and the two long tail feathers spread like the outside edges of a fan and outlined the distinctive harp-shaped feathers in the centre that had given him his name. And then he began to prance.

Tara could feel the rush of goose-bumps that covered her arms. A shivering perception of something magical and mystical, totally surreal, and Simon's eyes never left the bird's dance until he felt her glance at him.

The lyrebird shook his tail at them once more in a grand finale and then sauntered off into the bushes.

They stood silently, watching the bush where it had disappeared, but it had gone. Job done.

Simon looked amused and then strangely thoughtful. 'You know what this means?' Simon said quietly.

He watched her with an expression she didn't understand and she searched his face. Then remembered what he'd said weeks ago when he'd first arrived. But she wasn't saying that.

Simon sounded more spooked than excited. 'It's a sign.' He tilted his head. 'Which I didn't believe in before, I admit.' Then he shrugged and said lightly, as if sharing a joke, 'We must be meant for each other.'

She stared at him—couldn't believe that. More goose-bumps covered her arms at the thought. She and Simon? For ever? Nope. Couldn't happen. 'Or there's a gorgeous female lyrebird behind us that we can't see.'

He smiled but she had the feeling he was glad she'd poo-pooed it too. 'Could be that as well.'

Then he pulled her closer in his arms until they squeezed together and with the magic of the moment and the dusk slowly dimming into night, he kissed her and she kissed him back, and the magic settled over them like a gossamer cloud, but it wasn't quite the same, Simon wasn't quite the same, and when it was the moment that balanced between losing themselves or pulling back it was Simon who pulled back.

If she wasn't mistaken, there was look of poorly disguised anxiety on his face.

CHAPTER TEN

IN THE LAST glow of the dimming evening the motorbike's engine thrummed beneath them and Simon held onto Tara on the way back to the lake. A single beam of light swept the road-side and the rest was darkness, a bit like the bottom of the deepening hole of dread inside him. That had been too close. He wasn't ready for that kind of commitment. Sharing a lyrebird was for those who knew what they were doing.

Thank goodness she'd had the presence of mind to see his sudden distance because sud-denly he hadn't been sure he really wanted to step off the edge with Tara. When had it be-come more serious than he'd intended? Did she really feel the same and if she did could he trust himself to be everything she thought he was?

On the mountain, at the end, it had been Tara who had agreed they should go, agreed when Simon had said he was worried about hitting wildlife in the dark. But, despite the peculiar visions of lyrebirds scattering in the headlights, the real reason had been that he wasn't sure he was as heart-whole as he had been any more. In fact, he'd had a sudden onset of the heebie-jeebies about just how deep he was getting in here, and none of this was in his plans—or his belief system.

And then Tara had agreed so easily that now, contrarily, he'd decided she didn't feel secure either.

But earlier, standing with her in his arms, losing himself in the generosity that was Tara, despite her fierce independence, he'd almost believed the sudden vision that he could hold this woman for the rest of his days.

But what if he broke her heart for ever if he had to move on?

Like his mum had moved on from his dad. Like Maeve's man, and his ex-friend, had moved on from them. The problem was that since the lyrebird, just an hour ago, Simon felt connected to Tara by a terrifying concept he hadn't expected but which was proving stronger than he had felt with anyone in his world. And he wasn't sure he liked it.

She made him feel larger than life, which he wasn't, exuberant when he hadn't thought he had an exuberant bone in his body. She made him want to experience the adventure of the world. And with Tara it would be an adventure. A quest towards the kind of life he had only dreamt of having for himself.

Except it wasn't him.

He wasn't quite sure who she was seeing in him but it wasn't Simon Campbell. He needed to get a little distance back while he worked through this.

Because he wasn't the adventurous, fun guy

Tara needed. She needed someone to jump out of planes with, fall head over heels in love with her, and be there for the next month, the next year, the next lifetime. He couldn't be sure he could sign up for that.

She deserved someone who would do that. So why did he have the feeling there was a great cloud of foreboding hanging over his head?

Next morning at breakfast Maeve wandered into the kitchen and ducked under a Christmas streamer before she sat down. 'What's wrong with Simon?' She absently scratched her tummy and inclined her head back towards the bathroom her brother had just disappeared into.

The door slammed and Tara winced. 'No idea. He's been acting strange since we came back from the picnic last night.' Maybe he was always like this and she'd been too blinded by his pretty face.

Or she'd said something that made him realise she was the last woman he wanted to get involved with. *Suck it up, princess, you know this happens to you all the time.* 'Is he usually moody?'

'Nope.' Maeve shook her head. 'He's the most even-tempered of all of us. The only time he gets techy is if he's worried about something big.'

Did she qualify for big? Did he think she was trying to trap him? Cringe. Cringe.

Lord, no. She'd never do that. She'd been told often enough by Matron to push herself out there and be a little more demanding but it just wasn't in her make-up. If the family hadn't seen how badly she'd wanted their life, she hadn't been about to tell them and get knocked back for her pains.

She guessed Simon was that all over again. 'He'll get over it.' *And her.* Already had, it seemed. It was probably all in her imagination anyway and he had just been amusing himself.

Well, problem was there was so much to admire about him, and he seemed to enjoy her company, plus he was a darned good kisser, and she'd practically thrown herself at him last night and he'd knocked her offer back, and that had left them in an awkward place, now that she thought about it. Thanks very much, Simon.

Time to change the subject. And the focus of her life. 'So how are you going, Maeve?'

Simon's sister shrugged. 'I'm fine. Feeling less nauseous and much heavier around the middle.' She sent Tara one of the most relaxed smiles Tara had seen from her. 'But I'd rather talk about you two.'

Darn! Lulled into a false sense of security. 'There's no "us two".'

Maeve raised her brows disbelievingly and Tara wanted to bury her head in her hands. Seriously. How many other people thought she'd fallen for Simon? Or he for her? Just because they'd hung out together a bit, and kissed a few times, that smug voice inside insisted.

Maeve wasn't having any of that apparently. 'Well, if there's not a "you two" he's been pretty hopeless at getting the message across. What with parachuting photo packages, and pestering you for a bike ride, and Louisa for a picnic hamper—and the rug!'

Lots of eyebrow waggling coming her way here and Tara could feel the heat creep up her cheeks. So this was what it was like to have a sister.

Obviously Maeve had no scruples in laying stuff out in front of her and teasing. Maybe she hadn't been so unlucky as an orphan to avoid this stuff. Apart from Mick's sister, she'd never really been one for girly relationships. Again the idea of becoming fond of someone when you never knew when they'd go away for a weekend and never come back. She'd decided a long time ago it was better to keep her distance.

But Maeve wasn't keeping her distance, neither had she finished. 'Seems a lot of effort for someone he doesn't care about.'

Tara had no idea how to deal with this. With her acquaintances she'd just tell them to shut up but you couldn't do that to Maeve—or she didn't think it would work anyway. 'Can we change the subject?'

'Not until I give you some advice.'

Oh, no. 'Do you have to? Please. I hate advice. Comes with having to sort yourself out all your life.' She said it but now she knew Maeve better she doubted anything would stop her when she was on a roll. She almost wished for the washed-out, droopy dandelion Maeve had been before she'd recovered her spirits.

She looked again at the new, brighter Maeve and she knew she was happy her friend had found her equilibrium. Lyrebird Lake was doing its magic. So, no, she didn't wish for droopy Maeve back.

Over the last few weeks, gradually they had become friends, good friends, if she dared to say it. She and Maeve had found lots to smile about. Lots to agree and not agree about and quirky, girly conversations that had often little to do with Simon. And, at Maeve's request, nothing at all to do with Rayne, the father of Maeve's baby.

'Me? Not give advice?' Maeve laughed at her.

Tara sighed. 'But you're not having this all your own way. I'll listen to you if you tell me what you're thinking about Rayne.'

Maeve blinked in shock and Tara grinned. 'And if I have advice then you have to listen to me.'

Ha. Miss Bossy didn't like it so much in return. But to give Maeve her due, she sat back with a grimace. 'I was being pushy, wasn't I?' She shook her head and smiled wryly. 'You haven't seen this side of me yet but I'm not normally the pathetic wimp I've been since I came here.'

She looked around and then back at Tara. 'You know what? You're right. I do feel better since I came here. This place really is as amazing as Simon says it is.'

Tara looked around with fresh eyes. Made herself feel the moment. Smell the furniture polish. Taste the freshly brewed tea from the pot that Louisa had made before she'd gone out. Saw the little touches that spelt people cared. A Christmas nativity scene tucked in behind the bread basket. The growing pile of gifts under the tree. The photo frames of family that Louisa polished with her silver cloth every morning. 'I think it's the people.'

And Tara didn't ever want to leave but she wasn't expecting the world to be that perfect. 'Yep. It's amazing. And it is good to see you firing on all cylinders—even if you are a bit scary sometimes.'

'Scary? Me? You should meet my oldest sister, Kate.' Then Maeve showed she at least was focussed. 'Seeing that you hate advice, I'll keep it simple—and let you in on a secret.'

She sat forward, ready to impart her wisdom, and Tara pulled a face as she waited. 'My sisters and I have decided Simon's been hiding from a real romantic relationship all his life—he's terrified the fairy-tale isn't real.'

'Um. I hate to tell you this, but it isn't,' Tara said, but Maeve ignored her.

'Whether that came from our mother and his dad not staying together or the fact that he never knew his dad, we don't know.'

She lowered her voice. 'What we do know is that the right woman can help him come out from the place he's been hiding all these years—but she has to get past the barriers.'

'Barriers?' Tara was lost. She had no idea what Maeve was talking about. She hadn't noticed any barriers.

'Not when-you-meet-him barriers. He's too good a people person for that. It's later. Whenever a woman is getting close, he'd discover some other place that needed him more than he needed her and bolt. She'd try and hold him, he'd spend less time with her, and then she'd give up and drop him. I've seen it time and again. But you're different.'

Her? Tara? Different? She couldn't help the tiny glow of warmth the words left in her chest. Then she thought it through and decided there was another reason she was different. Maybe because she didn't expect people to want to look long term with her?

'He's scared of long term, Tara.'

Well, there you go. Maybe she was the right girl for him after all. She forced a smile. 'I'm not presuming long-term.' Had lost that expectation years ago.

'Might be the way to getting it.' Maeve looked at her.

That didn't make sense. 'You mean, actually say, *Hi, Simon, I don't expect long term*?' The fantasy was tragically attractive—but it was fantasy. But that didn't mean one day it mightn't happen. Did it?

Maeve waggled her brows. 'And that just might be the way to break through the barriers.'

Nope. Tara didn't understand and she backed away from reading anything ridiculously ambitious into Maeve's comments. 'Okay. I've listened.' And you are scaring the socks off me at the thought of having any such conversation with Simon. Although if Simon was scared she would try to trap him, he did need to know that wasn't in her plans.

But he had changed after the lyrebird, true, and he'd practically said he remembered what seeing the bird dance meant. True love and all that stuff. For a guy who wasn't thinking long term she guessed that could be scary. She wasn't scared, just didn't believe the hogwash. All too confusing for a conversation.

'Your turn.' She sat forward. 'Tell me about the father of your child.' She really did want to know. She couldn't imagine anyone leaving Maeve. She was gorgeous and funny, and she was classy.

Maeve's shoulders drooped. Her confident persona disappeared into the dejected woman Tara had first met. There was an extended silence and Tara thought for a moment Maeve was going to renege. Then she sighed. 'I fell for Rayne like a ton of bricks.' She lifted her head, her eyes unexpectedly dreamy, and remembered. 'He's a head taller than me, shoulders like a front-row forward, and those eyes. Black pools of serious lust when he looked at me. Which he did from across the room.'

Tara had to grin. Descriptive. 'Crikey. I'm squirming on my seat over here. So what happened?'

She shrugged. 'We spent the night together—then he went to jail.'

Tara remembered Maeve saying he'd omitted to tell her he was going to jail. 'Was he wrongly convicted?'

Tears filled Maeve's eyes. She chewed her lip and gathered her control. Then looked at Tara with a wry and watery smile. 'Thank you.'

Tara wasn't sure what was going on but she seriously wanted to get to the bottom of it. 'Did he tell you about it?'

Shook her head. 'Didn't have a chance. And since then he's refused to see or talk to me on the phone.'

That didn't make sense. 'So when did this happen?

Maeve patted her stomach. 'Eight months ago.'

O-o-o-kay. Tara suspected Simon might have reason to worry. 'And how long were you together before you fell pregnant?'

She sighed. 'One night. But I've always loved

Rayne. He was the bad boy all the girls lusted after. I always thought the problem was more his mum than Rayne—she was a single mum and couldn't kick her drug addiction—but despite our mum's misgivings he and Simon were always friends.'

And now he'd got Simon's sister pregnant on the way to jail. Probably why Simon wanted to wring his neck.

Maeve was still talking. 'Simon and he were mates through med school and then Rayne went to California to do paediatrics. And he was supposed to come and work with Simon at his hospital this year.'

She shrugged. 'Something happened when he was over there, and apparently as soon as he hit Australia alarm bells went off. Simon picked him up from the airport, and neither of us knew that the police would come for him as soon as he was back in the country. It seems he suspected it was a possibility and didn't tell us.'

'Wow. Seems a strange way to act.'

'I'm pretty sure he planned to tell but Simon got called out to a patient before he could, I think.' Maeve shrugged.

'Problem was, I've fancied this guy since I carried a lunchbox to school, hadn't seen him for eight years, and that night Simon left.' She shrugged. 'I was feeling low after a break-up, here was this guy coming I'd had a crush on since puberty and it all just happened. Except Simon has never forgiven him—when, in fact, the guy had little choice because I practically seduced him.'

Her face went pink and Tara could see a heck of a lot had happened. Wow again.

'Obviously I've thought about that night and I think Rayne's natural resistance was lowered by the fact he might be in prison for the next ten years and I was throwing myself at him.'

'Imagine?' Tara looked at Maeve. Gorgeous, sexy, and, she was beginning to suspect, wilful and a little spoilt, but in a nice way. A way

Tara could quite easily be envious of except she'd shaken that out of herself years ago as a destructive waste of wishful thinking.

'And then the next morning the police came and took him away. It was a shock because we'd slept together and he just walked away without looking back.'

Absently she stroked her belly. 'Simon was livid when he found out that Rayne had suspected they might come. But I think he'd come to explain and get advice from Simon, except it hadn't worked out. And then I complicated matters.'

Wow. Maeve had certainly complicated matters. It was like an end-of-season episode of a soap opera. Tara had major sympathy for Simon. But Maeve had problems too. And then there was the mysterious Rayne.

'Do you love him?'

She spread her hands. 'I've had all pregnancy to think about it. About the fact that he might not be the guy I think he is. Or if he was he might change a lot in prison. So when I see him again he might not be the hero that I always imagined him to be and I fell for the pretty face I'd always fancied and created the energy between us by wishful thinking.'

Tara agreed with her there. It all sounded explosively spontaneous. 'It's a possibility.'

'I know. I know. It was a whirlwind event that will affect the rest of my life. But really I don't know. He doesn't care enough to answer my calls. Or answer my letters. Or comment on the fact that I'm pregnant and soon to have his child. That hurts.'

Yep. That would hurt. 'That is hard.'

Maeve went on. 'When I found out I was pregnant I thought Simon was going to have a stroke. We had a huge fight. I said I was old enough to make my own mistakes and he said he could see that was true but not under his roof. Then he absolutely tore Rayne's actions

FIONA McARTHUR 197

to shreds when I knew it was mostly me. So we really haven't made up since then. But I still live under his roof so we've had sort of a cold truce for most of this year.'

She sighed again. 'I know I let him and my parents down. Crashed off my pedestal and that hurt too. But I swear, one look at Rayne, at his need for comfort, and I was a goner, and seeing how it turned out I can understand his reluctance to let me into his life now. I can regret the timing but if I'm ever going to have a child the fact that it's Rayne's is no real hardship.'

A can of worms getting wormier actually. 'I'm not sure I have advice for you. Except to say that guys in jail, even innocent ones, do change from the experience. I've known people who have. I'm not saying it won't work out between you, but he might be a harder, tougher man than the one who went in. If you do meet him again, which I guess you will if you're having his baby, make sure he is the man you love before you commit to anything. You have your baby to think of as well as yourself.'

Maeve looked back soberly. 'I guess it has been all about the baby and me. I do need reminding that Rayne is in a different world right now and that he's having it tough too. Thanks, Tara.'

Tara wasn't sure that was what she'd been trying to say. 'And thanks for your advice, though I can't see myself starting a conversation like that with Simon.' She smiled and stood up. 'As for your story, you make my life seem pretty boring.'

'Simon doesn't think you're boring.'

And here we begin the conversation again. Enough. 'The good news is I have to go and do some home visits so I'm going to leave you.' She carried her cup and saucer and cereal plate to the sink and rinsed them. 'Catch you later.'

As she walked towards her room she mulled over the conversation. No wonder Maeve had been low in spirits when she'd arrived. And it explained the tension between Simon and his sister.

It was understandable Simon felt betrayed by his friend and to a lesser degree by his sister. She'd actually love to hear Simon's side of the story but couldn't see how she could ask without betraying the confidence that Maeve had spoken to her about it all.

And that it all happened under his own roof wouldn't have helped his overactive protective bone.

Maeve had been very generous with her sharing and her advice and it had been nice to talk like that. Exchange banter with her friend. She was getting better at relationships with other people. Letting herself be more open and looking a little more below the surface to try to connect to other people instead of being too wary.

She'd never had a friend like Maeve before and hoped she'd helped her. Maeve had certainly given her something to think about with Simon. Maybe she could have real friendship relationships with women apart from being their midwife. Though she guessed she was Maeve's midwife as well.

She pulled on her jeans to ride the bike and slipped into her boots. Organised her workbag on autopilot and mulled over Maeve's words. Shook her head. He wasn't scared. Simon didn't care enough.

When they'd been together at the lookout he'd been a gentleman and not raised her expectations. She supposed it was a good thing but she really would have liked to lose herself all the way in those gorgeous arms. And he'd been such a good kisser. She shook her head. Come on. He was way out of her league. Get with the programme.

CHAPTER ELEVEN

SIMON STOOD IN the shower and could feel the edges of panic clawing at him. And he couldn't ease away by running back to Sydney Central work like he usually did because Maeve was getting close to having her baby. He had to be around in case anything happened.

This was certainly the time he usually left a relationship—way past it, in fact, as far as rapport between him and the woman went—except for the fact he would have been sleeping with her well and truly by now and that hadn't happened with Tara. How on earth had the emotional stuff happened when they hadn't even slept together? Everything was upside down. Back to front. And confusing.

Maybe it was proximity. Of course it was incredibly hard not to get closer than normal when you were living in the same house and working in the same place and associating with the same people.

Um, except he had lived with other women and not got too emotionally involved. And he had the horrible suspicion he'd miss Tara if he created the distance he needed—either mentally or geographically.

That was the scariest thing of all. It hadn't happened before. He'd always felt the relationship was well and truly over by the time he began to see the signs of long-term planning on the side of his lady friend. Which was a good thing because that way he wasn't responsible for hurting anyone.

But this was different. The unease fluttered again as he turned off the shower tap. Silly thoughts of birthday cakes in the future still made him smile but that was not the sort of thing to do if he was deep in a relationship with his next woman.

Listen to himself. He doubted he'd ever been deep into a relationship ever—more floating along the surface with good sex, and with women who were still his friends.

But right at this moment he was abstinent and sinking. No utopia after what had been a truly delightful afternoon yesterday with loads of potential—until that bloody lyrebird had said she was his true love and he'd panicked. Well, at least he had seen the danger before they'd completely consummated their relationship.

He combed his hair with his fingers and opened the steamy bathroom door. Oops. He'd been in here a while. But at least he'd come to some conclusion. All he needed to do was pull away. Create some distance and see how it felt.

His stomach rumbled and he headed for the kitchen as he continued to mull over his dilemmas.

He just needed to let Tara know subtly that he wasn't a long-term prospect and then maybe they could just be friends. As in platonic. Hmm.

That brought up a whole new set of unpleasant dilemmas. If he and Tara were just friends that meant she could have other friends who were men. Maybe a lover. Someone else to take on her adventures. Someone else to do what he had knocked back. Strangely, not funny, idea at all.

He needed to think about that one.

'Hi, Simon.' He looked up from his preoccupation and saw a jeans-clad goddess.

'Hi, Tara.' He felt a smile spread across his face and then fall away as his previous conversations with himself came back.

'You okay?'

'Sure.' Hitched his smile back up. 'Of course. You?'

'Fine.' He could feel her concern. Saw her shrug.

'Okay. I'm going for a ride. To see one of

my clients. Then maybe further afield. See you later.'

'Be safe.'

'High on my list. *Ciao.*'

He called after her, 'I didn't know you spoke Italian?'

'I don't.' She stopped. '*Ciao* and food items. Pizza, lasagne, *boccioni*.' She shrugged. 'The extent of my Italian. Anyway. See you.'

'Bye. When are you back?'

She stopped again and sighed. 'No idea.'

He opened his mouth to ask something else and closed it again. What was he doing? He lifted his hand to wave and turned away.

Geez. He was hopeless.

'Simon?' He spun back and she was there. Just behind him. And she was chewing on those gorgeous lips in a way that he wanted to touch her mouth with his fingers to stop her damaging anything.

'It's okay, Simon. I'm not expecting long term,

you know. I'll be moving on soon.' She shook her head. 'Just wanted to let you know.'

'Me too,' he said helplessly.

And then she spun on her heel and walked away quickly. He was still staring after her when he heard the bike start and the roar as she rode away.

So why didn't he feel better? Basically she was saying they could have fun with no strings. Right up his alley. And he'd told her he felt the same. Liar.

When Tara drove into the driveway late in the afternoon of the next day Simon was sitting out at the manger, watching the animals.

She swung her helmet on her finger as she walked across the springy grass Louisa loved to water, and the smile he gave as she approached made the slight trepidation she'd started with worth the effort.

'Looking particularly fetching there, Miss Tara.'

He sounded relaxed. Thank goodness for that. Until she'd given herself a stern talking to she'd been replaying the video of the dumb things she'd said in her head before she'd left. Dumb because she hadn't needed to put them out there, though he'd agreed—not dumb because she hadn't meant them, because she had. She sat down beside him on the bench and looked at the manger. 'Hi, Simon.'

'And what did you do today?'

She opened her eyes wide. 'I've had a very nice day, thank you. I visited my two postnatal mums, then rode all the way to the lighthouse. Watched the parachutists float from the sky. It was very beautiful.' Politely. 'What did you do?'

'I did a couple of hours for Dad in the general hospital while he took Mia to the airport to go visit a sick friend, and I had a decadent snooze this afternoon because I didn't sleep well last night.' He watched her face. 'I guess you're tired now?'

She looked at him over the top of sunglasses. 'No, Mr Old Man. I'm not tired. I am young and enthusiastic for adventure at all times.'

'Goody.' He grinned. 'And for the record that's the second time you've called me an old man.'

'Well, stop acting like one.'

He didn't offer any answers to that one. 'Trouble is I'm wide awake after my nap and could party all night. Got any ideas?'

She shrugged. 'What sort of things? Nature? Dining? Dancing? Astronomy?'

'Ah. Astronomy has potential.'

'For what?'

'Seeing stars.'

'I could help you with that right now.' She swung her helmet thoughtfully. He was teasing and it was fun. Until he said, 'I wondered if you were into violence.'

She thought about some of the people she

knew and the way their demons seemed to lead them to violence. The fun went out of it and she stood up. They were from such different worlds. 'Nope. Much prefer to just walk away.'

She saw him reach out to stop her and then drop his hand and his mixed signals only confused her more.

Then he said, 'Sorry. I don't know what I said but I don't want to ruin the mood. So, before you go, what I've really been doing is sitting here waiting to ask you to dinner. Louisa and Maeve have gone to Dad's to stay overnight and mind the girls. I'd like to get dressed up and go on a date with you to the new restaurant down by the lake.'

She sat down again. 'Oh.' She looked at him. 'A date?'

'A fun date with a lady I like spending time with.'

She thought about that one. 'Fun', meaning 'not serious'. Wasn't that what she'd said she wanted, too? Hadn't they both agreed on that yesterday morning? 'Sure. I'd like that. What time?'

'When you're ready. I made a booking for six-thirty for seven.' She raised her brows at his presumption but he was ahead of her. 'It's not heavily booked and they don't mind if I cancel.'

She grinned at him. 'You really are a thoughtful man.'

'We old guys are like that.'

'I don't really think you're old.' She looked him over with mischief in her eyes. 'Far too sexy for an old guy.'

'Keep thinking that way. I thought we could have a drink before dinner at the bar, if you don't mind walking there.'

'Thank you. Sounds nice.' She glanced at her watch. 'I'd better have a shower and get changed, then.'

'No rush.'

'Sure. But I like to be on time. I was brought up that way.'

Simon watched her walk away, that sexy, determined little walk that had him squirming on his seat. And the crazy thing was she had no idea what she did to him. He wasn't much better at guessing why she affected him like she did but tonight he'd come to the conclusion he was going to try to figure it out by taking it to the next level. Regardless of the risk.

The new restaurant was built on a little knoll overlooking the lake. The grounds were surrounded by a vibrant green hedge with a latched gate. The entry had been landscaped into lots of little rock pools and greenery with a wide wooden boardwalk winding through to get to the restaurant door. There was even a little bridge they had to climb up and over and Tara couldn't keep the smile off her face. 'This is gorgeous. I can't believe it's here and I didn't know.'

'They've only just opened. Mia told me about it when I asked her where I should take you.'

She looked at him. Surprised. 'You told Mia we were going on a date?'

'That's what she said.'

Tara laughed. 'Your family is funny.' And gorgeous, but that was okay. She had settled a lot since her ride that afternoon. Decided that clarity came with enjoying the moment, not worrying about it. She was here with Simon now, and she was going to have a wonderful evening. 'I'm starving.'

'Excellent.'

They started with drinks at the bar, and behind the barman a huge window overlooked the water and showcased the sunset, and to the left a narrow curving terrace gave the diners a water view while they ate.

He watched Tara sigh with pleasure as she

took a sip of her pina colada and gazed around. 'This place is amazing.'

You're amazing. He followed her gaze. Took in the colours on the lake. 'It is great.' He saw it through Tara's shining eyes and acknowledged that he hadn't let it soak in. He had been so busy with his thoughts and plans and second-guessing his own emotions he was missing the pleasure. Vowed to stop that right now. Vowed to enjoy the pleasure of company with the woman he wanted to be with—and be like Tara and enjoy things, without worrying about tomorrow. Imagine that!

It was easier than he expected when he tried it. Everything seemed suddenly brighter. Wow.

'How's your drink?'

She pretended to look at him suspiciously. 'Why? You want some?' So then he laughed. Because it was funny.

'No, I don't want some, Miss I'm-Not-Sharing. I have my own drink. Though mine doesn't look as flashy as yours, with its slice of pineapple and pretty pink umbrella.'

She grinned. 'Good. I've never had one before. And I like umbrellas.' She offered him her straw. 'But you can have a sip if you really want.'

I'll sip later, he thought, and suddenly the night was alive with promise and joy, and the conversation took off as he let go of worrying about the past and the future and just experienced Tara's company.

They flowed from the bar to their table, the most private one he could acquire, and the sun went down, as did the glorious seafood and the delightful sparkling wine in the bottle.

By the time he paid the bill they were both pleasantly mellow, and he had no hesitation in capturing her hand in his for the walk home around the lake.

The lake path from the restaurant to the hospital and Louisa's house was lit by yellow globes that matched the moon and it was almost as bright as day as they ambled along.

This time when there was a rustle in the bushes Tara just smiled at the noise and carried on walking.

He glanced back to where the undergrowth still crackled. 'So you're not afraid of snakes in the bushes now?'

'Nope.' She squeezed his hand. 'I'm going to believe it's a lyrebird who can sound like a motorbike. If he wants to, of course.'

'Of course.' And Simon realised he had become decidedly more trusting about other facets of lyrebird lore. He stopped and she stopped too. He pulled her by the hand until she faced him and lifted his fingers to her cheek. 'You look like a lake princess in the moonlight.'

She glanced up at the moon and the angles of her face shone like those of a perfectly carved silver goddess with the reflection of the moonlight shining Tara's truth at him.

She was frowning at him, trying to read him, and goodness knew what was flashing across his face as his mind raced, because she looked a little unsure. 'Thank you for the compliment. I like moonlit nights the best. Never been keen on the dark.'

He just wanted to hold her safe and never let her go. One day he would ask why she preferred to have a moonlit night than a dark one. Hopefully he would have the chance to ask.

He leant in and kissed her gently because if he did it properly he wouldn't be able to stop and she didn't deserve that, but she lifted her hands up and held his head there.

Tara kissed him back with a warmth and generosity he remembered from the lookout and for a few minutes there he forgot his good intentions. Until they heard some people coming along the path and he put her away from him.

That's right. He had no intention of seducing Tara in a park. 'Let's go home now.'

* * *

There was something in the way he said '*home now*' that sent a whisper of promise across Tara's skin. Home. Together. Now. That last kiss had been different, wonderful and absolutely intoxicating. Lucky Simon had heard the people coming because she'd been deaf to the world.

They were walking quite fast now. Seemed he'd decided caution was overrated and that was okay. Seriously okay because, no matter what, she wanted to sleep with this gorgeous, sexy, kind man at least once. She was not going to regret not spending time with Simon for the rest of her life. It might be her last chance.

Louisa and Maeve had gone to Mia's so they would be alone and that removed that last of her resistance, if she'd had any.

Simon held her hand tightly as they walked even more quickly along the lit path. She resisted the urge to run.

CHAPTER TWELVE

SIMON PUSHED OPEN the door and Tara reached up to turn on the lights but he stilled her hand.

'Can you see in the moonlight?'

Her hand fell away from the switch and instinctively they both slowed to draw out the moment. Tara's eyes adjusted and she could see easily as she stared into the strong features above her, cherished the fact that Simon found her very attractive, could almost feel herself unfurling in front of him. The silly, exciting, headlong rush to get here was completed and now it was time to savour their first moments.

Okay. Settle. Slow your breathing. Just soak it in.

He drew her to him, leaned in and brushed her mouth with his. Brushed again. Gently pulling on her lip with his teeth. A mingling of breath and promise and introduction to a Simon she didn't know. One she liked very much.

'You taste so beautiful.'

'Pina colada?'

'The taste of Tara. I like it.' He kissed her again.

'Mmm.' Closed her eyes at his reverence because it made her want to cry and he might think she did so for the wrong reasons. 'I like you tasting me.' Just a little bit gruffly.

He smiled, a brief flash of teeth in the moonlight, and then he was pulling her slowly down the hallway to his room. She wanted to lose herself like she had on the path, but she wanted to savour every moment, store up every stroke of his fingers as his hand trailed down her arm.

They passed her door. Good choice, she thought mistily. 'My room's a mess.'

'Mine's too tidy. I'm sure we'll find something in common.' He bent his body and slid one arm under her shoulder, the other behind her knee, and lifted her easily into his arms and against his chest. 'Something along the lines of I like to hold you in my arms and you like to be carried.'

'Not something I had previously been aware of.' She laid her head back and savoured it. 'It seems you're right.'

He squeezed her to him. Paused at his door. 'Will you spend the night with me, Tara?'

'That sounds very nice, Simon.'

He gave a small deep chuckle as he pushed open his door and closed it behind them. Then he stood her up in front of the bed and reached around behind her to ease the zipper down her back. A long leisurely unzipping that promised much.

He curved the fabric off her shoulders until it slithered into a heap at her feet, a rumpled puddle of material, then helped her step out. She looked back at this gorgeous man, burnished by the gentle light, and decided he looked like a magnificent knight as he stood in front of her. One who deserved something a little more romantic than her serviceable underwear but there wasn't much she could do about it except wish for a second she'd bought the lacy set she'd scorned last week.

Then Simon lifted her hands to his neck and traced them down his chest so that she too could undo fastenings, liking that she could follow his lead and lose the awkwardness of her lack of skill at this slow dance of undressing.

Surprisingly easily, she unfastened buttons until his shirt flapped open and she couldn't help an indulgent exploration of the ridges and hollows and bands of rippled muscles that she'd ached to stroke all evening—and while she was there she undid the silver buckle of his belt—such an unclick of commitment that made her smile a slow, wicked, womanly smile.

She felt his breath draw in as she slipped open

the button of his trousers and carefully eased the teeth of his zip over the unmistakable bulge of his erection.

His fingers slid up her back and then around her neck and over her throat so she tilted her head, first a gentle brush of his lips over her throat and then a searing kiss that clouded her vision and had her matching the sudden flurry of movements they both made to remove the last of the clothing between them.

He lifted her again, placed her reverently like a prize across his bed and knelt down beside her, naked in the moonlight, a beautiful gilded warrior to claim his trophy.

The moonlight flooded across them, silvery streams of light with dark stripes where the branches from the tree outside blocked it, so when he lay down beside her the light rippled across his skin from silver to shadow and back to silver again.

She must have been in the stripes too, because he said softly, 'You still look like a mystical creature from the lake.'

'There's no mystery. Just me.'

He gathered her into his arms. Squeezed her to him. 'There's no "just" about you, Tara.'

And then he began to kiss her. Worship her. Inch by inch, kiss by kiss, stroke by stroke, accompanied by whispered murmurs of delight, discoveries that were marvelled over, and sudden indrawn breaths on Tara's side as she too discovered there was another world, a whispering, wonderful, wild world of worship at the hands of Simon Campbell.

As the sun peeped fingers of light towards the tangle of sheets on the bed Simon looked down at the woman he held in his arms. The warmth of sudden knowledge broke through to him like a beam from the dawn. Like an epiphany. No warning. Just a moment in time between touching and looking—then he realised that, of course, he loved her! Had done for days. Fool!

Tara was the one. It had been building since the lookout. And he'd denied it, the incredible dance of the lyrebird that had warned him about the truth.

Instead of panic, the relief was overwhelming because his body had been shouting in his ear for the last torturous days and he'd been talking it down. Saying they didn't know each other well enough, he couldn't possibly, but that feeling of delight every time he'd seen her should have warned him. Well, he knew her now, in the biblical sense, and that was what it had taken for him to know, without a doubt, that he'd fallen in love.

Simon tightened his hands around the waist he'd cradled through the night. The satin skin he'd held in his arms and stroked with wondering hands. Kissed the tiny intricate rose tattooed on her shoulder. He just knew there would be a story about that.

Making love with Tara had been everything it had never been with anyone else.

A revelation, a slow and gentle exploration that had seen her unfurl like the tail of the lyre-bird, he thought whimsically, into a slow mesmerising dance of magnificent generosity that had enraptured them both. She gave it all, held nothing back, and knowing her past only made him more exultant about her generosity.

The trouble was, now he knew he loved her, what he didn't know was if she loved him. All he could do was pray that Tara would see the same thing.

Prickly, determined, independent little Tara, and he discovered that when he loved, the feeling just grew, shifted, touched the whole world with its glow, irrevocably, from the depths of his soul, and there was no going back. So this was what his father had meant when he'd said it would happen one day and he'd recognise it.

He couldn't believe it. His sisters would be in whoops of laughter. His mother would be thrilled he was thinking of settling down.

Settling down?

That was why everything was so upside down and back to front. So unlike it usually was because he'd never fallen in love before. He was in love with Tara. No wonder he hadn't recognised it.

The last time Tara woke, because there had been several awakenings in more ways than one, Simon wasn't holding her and she felt the loss like a piece of herself was gone. And her heart began to pound. What would happen today?

Nothing or everything? Would he be kind but distant? Would he be loving and different towards her? She hugged herself and assured her newly awakened inner woman that everything would be fine, no matter what. But she didn't believe it.

Thankfully, before she could whip herself into too much of a state Simon poked his head around the door. The smile on his face wasn't distant at all. Actually, his eyes said he wanted to jump in beside her and she was tempted to crook her finger at him. 'Your breakfast awaits you on the back veranda, my lady.'

She sat up. Realised she was naked. Clutched the sheet and blushed as Simon enjoyed the view with a decidedly proprietorial glint in his eye. 'Maeve and Louisa will be home soon, the girls leave for school in five minutes, and I thought you might like to get dressed before then.'

Absolutely. Crikey. 'Yes. Please.' She waved him away and he pulled his head back but not before he winked at her like a villain in a farce. Well, it didn't seem as though Simon regretted the night.

The tension slid from her shoulders and several unlimbered muscles twinged as she swung her feet out of the bed. Her cheeks heated as she caught a glance of a thoroughly sated woman in the mirror, and she tried one of Simon's winks on herself. She grinned. Felt silly.

But there was a curve to her lips she couldn't seem to move and she slid the same shirt around her shoulders that she'd removed from Simon last night, sniffed the collar, and recognised the faint cologne she would always associate with him, then gathered her own clothes with one hand and clutched the edges of the shirt together with the other hand as she let herself out of the room and into her own.

The fastest gathering on record of clothes for the day and then she was safely behind the bathroom door before anyone else arrived home.

By the time she was out, dressed and confident, on the outside at least, Louisa and Maeve were home. Maeve was trying desperately to catch her eye but she refused to collide with the knowing looks that kept coming her way and Simon was whistling and avoiding his sister as well.

Diversion was needed. 'How are the girls?'

Louisa seemed oblivious to the undercurrents in the room. Thank goodness somebody was. 'As prettily mannered as you could wish for.' Louisa sighed blissfully. 'I do enjoy their company. And they're so excited about the carols tonight.'

'That's right. The carols by candlelight.' Tara was pretty excited about that too. She'd be with Simon. She wondered if he'd hold her hand in front of his family. The thought was nerve-racking and she stuffed it away to peek at later. 'What time does Mia get home?'

'Angus picks her up from the airport at lunchtime so she'll be back before they finish school.'

It was so weird having a normal conversation. Especially with Simon watching her. She could feel him. And then there were Maeve's eyes nearly bugging out of her head with curiosity. She tried to concentrate on Louisa. 'I've got two home visits this morning but can help any other time if you need me to do something.'

The older lady smiled serenely. 'Thanks, Tara. I'll let you know.'

Tara nodded and followed Simon out to the veranda, where he'd set a place and made her favourite herbal tea and raisin toast. He stood behind her chair and pushed it in when she sat down. Every time she glanced at him she could feel her cheeks heat. And her belly glow. Finally understanding the preoccupation a woman could have with sleeping with her man. Was Simon her man? He leaned across and kissed her and then he sat opposite and calmly sipped his tea.

Maeve arrived, hovered and Tara had a way to go before she reached that skill of composure Simon had. Sipped her tea, ate half a piece of toast and decided to bolt. She rose. 'I've got to go.'

The words sounded abrupt but Simon only smiled at her. Gave her a wink. Maeve looked thwarted and Tara decided exit had been an excellent idea as she walked hurriedly back into the house to get her gear, and knew the rest of the day would require some concentration if she wasn't going to end up staring into space every few minutes with a silly smile on her face.

Carols by candlelight began as the sun set. Angus and Simon had taken the trailer full of chairs and set them up to the left of the stage. It was a warm, sleeveless type of evening and the children were dressed in pretty red dresses and short-legged Santa helper suits, with Santa hats and flashing stars, and dozens of little battery-powered candles to wave in the darkening evening as families from all over the valley began to arrive.

Simon had been to the shops and Tara had never had so many Christmas-themed trinkets in her possession.

Her favourite was a long silver wand with a star on top that glowed silver in the darkening sky. Though the Christmas headband with reindeer made her laugh and the earrings shaped like Christmas trees that flashed on and off and matching bracelet were all very cool. When she'd demurred, Simon had laughed and said she could give them away if she had too much but he hadn't been able to resist buying them because every time he'd seen something new he'd thought she would like it.

Tara liked it. She'd never bought herself anything festive, had thought they were all for little children, but Simon said she looked like a Christmas angel so she hugged them to herself when what she wanted to do was hug Simon.

In the distance the lights from Louisa's house shone merrily and the carols began with a rousing rendition of 'Good King Wenceslas', and Tara turned with amazement as Simon began to sing in a deep, hilarious baritone that, despite his intention to make her smile, was incredibly rich and tuneful.

She had never thought she could ever be this happy, this excited, this included in a family night like tonight, and she shook her head at the gorgeous man beside her as he took her hand in his and hugged her to him.

She saw Louisa smile at them, and even Angus looked across at them warmly. Mia winked and Maeve grinned at her every time she saw them.

Tara was in love!

The day before Christmas Eve and Tara turned over in bed. Last night had been amazing. Simon had seemed so proud of her, so happy to show everyone that he cared, and just soaking up the night with Simon's arm around her had been one of the most magical evenings she'd ever had.

She was in love but instead of waking in the golden glow she should have, it was the terrified child from the orphanage who woke, and she felt like scooting down the hallway and crawling into Simon's bed for reassurance. She really, really hated that horrible feeling it was all too good to be true.

All those times as a kid when she'd thought maybe she could fall in love with a family, had waited for the call that only other children seemed to get—this was much worse, a thousand times worse.

What if something happened to this precious feeling between her and Simon?

To make it more terrifying, he was a part of the most amazing family of them all. A whole Christmas fairy-tale and Santa Claus stocking of loving people that she would give anything to be a part of. Could she possibly believe that good things like that could happen to her? She thought of the lyrebird and a little calmness came out of nowhere. Maybe she just needed to learn to believe it?

And then her phone rang, probably a mum with an unsettled baby, just as she was about to get out of bed and dress for work. It took her a moment to recognise the voice from her past. Mick.

That was when she knew it was the end.

She felt shock, and horror, and a queer almost relief from the impending doom she'd worried so much about. Karma-wise she'd probably talked herself into this bad luck. 'How did you find my number?'

'I didn't just find your number.' The smug tone sent icy shivers down her back. Not for herself. She wasn't afraid of Mick, or not much except when he was off his face on some substance, but she was afraid for Louisa getting a nasty shock when she opened the door. Or

Maeve. For anyone else who got in his way. More afraid of the look of disgust when the people she cared about in Lyrebird Lake saw that she was the reason he was there.

Mick's gravelly voice recalled her to the present. 'I want my bike, Tara.'

The darned bike. 'The bike is mine. You owed me a lot more than it's worth.'

'It's mine. And I'm coming for it. And that's not all I'm coming for. You and me, Tara. Like old times.'

Like hell. He really was high. She glanced at the clock. 'Where are you?'

'Leaving Sydney soon.'

She didn't know what to do. What to think. Had to stall until she came up with a plan to keep Mick away from Lyrebird Lake and everyone in it until she could sort it.

She was crystal clear in her mind that she'd accepted the bike wasn't worth it. Thankfully she had grown beyond defining herself because of a possession and was over her need to have a win over Mick for her self-esteem. If she wasn't so angry with him for risking her new-found friendships, let alone the precious jewel of her relationship with Simon, she'd feel sorry for Mick.

Even in her fog of anguish Tara could see he was missing out in life because of his bitterness about the past. But feeling sorry for Mick had led her into this mess of debt and negativity in the first place.

But she was slowly climbing out of that hole. Mentally she already had, and financially she was in the process, one small payment at a time.

And now, being with Simon had helped her find another stronger and prouder layer of herself. She was someone a wonderful man admired, and she could leave here a better person because of that.

The sigh that accompanied the thought seemed to tear itself loose from her soul. Because she would have to leave now that Mick had found her. Not with him, but after him, because he'd just keep coming back every time he wanted to extort something.

'You could pay me ten thousand dollars' worth of debts and it's all yours.'

Mick laughed and it wasn't a pleasant sound and Tara grimaced. He was high on something. 'You'll never get the money but I will get my bike. I know where you live. I'm coming to have Christmas with all your little families. I've seen the house where you live on Google Earth. Bet they don't know about me. But they will.'

'I'm negotiable on the bike, Mick. But there were never *old times* between you and me. Just a short time. I was your friend and you let me down. Nothing else is on the agenda.'

'What's up, Tara? You too good for your orphan buddies now?'

'The blood-sucking ones. Yes. I have a new

life. One I've worked hard for. You're not a part of it.'

'That's what you think.'

'Forget it, Mick. I'll give you the bike, and you can get lost. But you can't have it now. I'm working this morning and don't finish until late this afternoon. I'll meet you tonight.'

Blow. That was family night at Mia and Angus's. 'About six.' The whole family was meeting for drinks to be there when the girls went to bed. Apparently they did it every year. She would just have to cry off and meet Mick somewhere out of sight while they all went on and had dinner.

Though how she'd smuggle the bike out of town would be tricky. That was the problem with Harleys. It wasn't like they didn't have a distinctive sound. Even lyrebirds noticed the noise. She'd say she had to go out for one of her women. Early labour. Simon would believe that. Except now she was lying to him. But she couldn't help that.

And then Mick upped the stakes. 'Nope. Think I'll spend Christmas in Lyrebird Lake. Seems like as fine a place as any. With my good friend Tara.'

Tara felt a clutch of dread. What if she couldn't stop him? If it was too late? The cold wind of the real world was blowing through her life again. She could imagine the children frightened of Mick, Simon sticking up for her and Mick fighting him, Louisa terrified. Nightmare in Lyrebird Lake and she had to stop it all before any of it could happen.

She needed to stall him. Stop him the only way she could think of. 'If you come anywhere near my friends, my work or my home before I say so, I'll douse the bike in petrol and burn it.' Her voice lowered and she put every ounce of conviction she could muster into the threat. 'You know I will.'

A pause and then a bluster. 'You won't have the chance.'

'Try me.' There was a silence. 'Only on my terms and until then…leave me alone. Give me until tonight to figure something out. I'll meet you somewhere away from here and hand it over. Ring me around six some time but I don't want you in this town. Or I will destroy the bike.'

That morning at work Tara found it incredibly difficult to concentrate. She kept imagining Simon's face if he came face to face with wild-eyed Mick, who looked even worse than he was, except when he was high, and he really was a bad man. Why on earth anyone would tattoo their face was beyond Tara, though she didn't regret the tiny rose on her own shoulder, remembrance for the tragically short life of Mick's sister.

Maybe if she hadn't gone with Mick for that

first tattoo he wouldn't have started painting his body but she would never know. The past was the past.

She just wished the past and the people from it would stay there! Especially now she'd glimpsed a future she'd foolishly thought she had a chance at.

The ward was quiet. They'd had a peaceful birth earlier in the day, one of Mia's mothers, and Tara spent the day sitting beside the new mum, gently praising her early breastfeeding skills. Everything was tidy and she was thinking she might even get off a little early when the phone rang to say her last due woman was coming in.

For the first time in her career she wished a baby would wait.

Of course, it didn't.

Tara didn't get home at three like she wanted, to give herself time to get organised. She arrived home at ten to six and Maeve and Louisa were busy in the kitchen, making finger food for tonight's family get-together at Mia's.

Simon had been out all day apparently, shopping, which was a good thing because every time someone spoke to her she jumped and he would notice more than anyone that she was preoccupied and nervous.

When she picked up her phone from her room she grimaced at all the missed calls. When she tried to return the call on Mick's mobile, his phone was turned off and she felt unease crawl up her neck. Missing his calls wouldn't leave Mick in a good frame to negotiate with.

Frustration gnawed at her. She needed to get in contact before he took matters into his own hands.

What if he was already in town? What if he knocked on the door and frightened Louisa? Or her greatest fear, picked a quarrel with Simon?

Tara quickly typed in a message. Gave directions to a place safely away from the town. Tried to imply he couldn't come to the lake but without him knowing he had her worried. This was her worst nightmare and she threw on her jeans and grabbed her helmet.

Behind her eyes a dull throb of tiredness and strain made her gulp the water beside her bed in the hope it would help the headache, and she stared through the curtains to the street as she drank.

Hell. Damn. Blast it. This was so unfair. She didn't deserve this imploding of her dream town. She felt like pulling her hair and stomping her feet. But that had never been her way so she drew a deep breath and straightened. It didn't matter about her. It was the people at the lake who mattered and she needed to stop Mick from upsetting them. A sudden vision of Mick and Simon fighting made nausea rise in her throat.

Just before she left, one last attempt as she paused in the hallway, she finally managed to get through to Mick. And as she'd dreaded, he'd borrowed a friend's car and trailer and had stopped for petrol only an hour away.

The dinner started at six-thirty and Tara estimated it would take her an hour to get to Mick, hand over the bike and get home.

Simon had gone to the next big town, shopping with his father, and still wasn't back so at least she could get away.

Tara repeated the directions to the local rubbish dump, on the inbound side of town, she could hand over the bike and walk the four miles home without anyone seeing her.

She had no idea what she'd say when everyone realised the bike was gone but that was the least of her worries. She'd just say she'd had to give it back.

CHAPTER THIRTEEN

SIMON HAD HAD a great day with his dad, had spent most of his time buying quirky gifts for Tara, and couldn't wait to hug her after a day with her filling his mind.

Then he saw Tara standing in the hallway talking on the phone. She hadn't seen him and he stood quietly and soaked in the vision. The light shone on her spiky silver hair, which exposed her gorgeous neck, and he wanted to trace that faint line behind her ear. Kiss that spot where her pulse beat gently against his mouth. He'd done a lot of that the other night. That hadn't been all he'd done and somehow they hadn't been able to recapture a moment when they could be together, alone, since then. He needed to do something about that.

She looked so good he wanted to drag her off to his room and have his wicked way with her right then and there but he guessed he'd have to wait until they could get away.

She'd finished the call so he moved towards her. 'Hi, Tara. Looking forward to tonight?' She jumped, and it wasn't a little one, it was a full-blown knee-jerk fright, and his own heart rate accelerated.

'Sorry.' He frowned, noticed the strain in her face he hadn't seen before, then remembered she'd been at work today. Not a good day? He knew how that felt.

He reached out and touched her shoulder with the idea of maybe sharing a little hug and she jumped again. Looked at him and then away and none of it was encouraging. What was going on? 'You okay?'

He tried to catch her eye but she turned her head. Now he was worried. Maybe she regretted the other night. He hoped not. He glanced at her jeans and boots. 'You going out on the bike?'

'Home visit. Early labour. Probably miss the dinner.'

Bummer. He'd been really looking forward to cuddling up to Tara while they all sat around and toasted the season. He guessed this had happened to all of his previous girlfriends and now the boot was on the other foot. 'Who is it? Want me to come? I could sit outside and reassure the man of the house.'

'You don't know her and, no, I don't want you to come.' A quick hunted glance and he was beginning to wonder if this was bigger than he thought.

Now what did he say? She looked like she was going to cry. 'You sure everything is okay?'

He watched her do that calming thing she did, a big breath, dropping the expression from her face, easing the tension from her shoulders. What had he done to make her that tense?

She shook her head. 'I'll see you later, Simon.'

And that was that. 'Okay.' Not a lot he could do about it except stalk her and that wasn't his style. 'I'll tell Mia you got called out.'

'Just leave it. I'll tell her.' She smiled but it wasn't one that made him feel good. 'Apologise for me. Maybe I'll get there before it all finishes, maybe not. Have a good night.'

'Sure.' He was anything but sure. Watched her go. But the feeling of unease glowed in his gut as he heard the sound of the bike start up. If he didn't know better he'd swear she'd looked panic-stricken for a minute there. Something was going on and he knew Tara well enough to suspect she was unhappy about where she was going. So why would that be? What could possibly make Tara unhappy about going to one of her women in labour? A poor domestic situation? Surely not. If that were the case she'd take someone else because that was the protocol. What if one of her women had a violent partner? Simon wished he'd asked a bit more. The unease grew in his gut and he decided to walk to Mia's and ask her if she knew anything.

Tara blinked back her tears. The wind on her face was achingly familiar and the throb of the engine hummed goodbye. Tara gained little enjoyment from her last ride but she was past lamenting over the loss.

She'd lied to Simon. To his face. But she couldn't see any other way of protecting those she'd come to love. Yes, she loved Simon, she loved Louisa, she loved every darned person in Lyrebird Lake, it seemed, and all the sighs and shoulder drops in the world weren't going to lighten that load.

She'd let them down. And now she was going to sign away her only possession in the world to stop them finding out about her past, but she couldn't help feeling it wasn't going to stop disaster happening anyway.

She turned off the main road onto the quiet gravel road to the tip. It was good it was quiet because she really didn't want anyone from Lyrebird Lake wondering why she was driving this way at this time of the evening.

And maybe that was why she came round the corner just a little too fast. Hit a patch of gravel just a little bit deep.

And for the first time lost control of the big bike as the front wheel skidded in the gravel and went sideways. Tara fought to stay upright, fought the urge to hit the brake, skidded sideways up the road valiantly upright but at a dangerous angle. As the bike slowed she managed to stay upright and slowed more until she thought she'd manage to correct the angles in the end.

She concentrated, fiercely willing the front wheel to straighten as she pulled it around, but her luck ran out because she'd run out of straight road and didn't make the bend. She hit the grass and flew into the scrub until the bike caught on a strong branch and jerked to a stop, where it fell with lack of forward motion and went down, with Tara frantically shifting her bottom leg so she wouldn't be pinned underneath. Her ankle jerked and caught and she pulled frantically to get it clear and the pain shot up her leg as it twisted.

She could feel her heart racing in her ears. Tara pulled herself backwards on her bottom until she was clear of the bike as its massive weight sank slowly closer and closer to the ground, crushing the undergrowth with a sizzling crackle, until it was lying flat on its side. Tara's back came up against the trunk of a tree she was very glad to have missed. Her ankle throbbed but she wasn't trapped under the bike. Still some good to be found.

But she had no idea how she was going to lift the deadweight of the bike to get it off the ground.

After a minute of gathering her nerves, Tara

crawled from her position against the tree and stood gingerly upright to brush herself off. She put a little weight on her ankle; it wobbled but stayed upright with a low-level throbbing. It could have been a lot worse.

At least she'd had jeans on. She'd refused to wear her leathers and walk home in them, but she hadn't escaped unscathed. As well as scratches on her arms as she and the bike had barrelled through the bushes, the areas where the stressed jeans had parted had let in tiny scratches and stings that would be annoying but not kill her. Her biggest dilemma was that she needed to get the bike upright and beat Mick to the rubbish dump before he decided she wasn't coming and head to Lyrebird Lake anyway.

She pulled her phone from her pocket and tried Mick's number but he wasn't answering. Peered at her watch but the screen was broken and she had to pick the plastic out to be able to read the numbers. It must have happened as she'd come through the bushes. She had ten minutes until she was supposed to be there.

She took a big, deep breath as she struggled to stand the bike while putting all of her weight on one leg. Ouch! No luck. Tara tried from the other side.

Pull! No luck, just a twinge of discomfort in her back from the effort and a fiercer ache from her ankle. She walked back again to the lifting side and tried jamming a stick as a lever to get it up. The stick broke.

No luck. She'd known it was going to be an unequal contest. It was all very well to sit astride a big bike. Even pulling it off its stand was fine when she was balanced evenly on her feet. But to lift a heavy motorcycle that was deadweight from lying on its side on the ground was just too much for her to achieve on her own. Even swearing was an effort after the last superhuman effort she'd made to no avail.

It was getting dark. She tried Mick again but

he still wasn't answering his phone. The road was deserted, a fact she'd been happy about a few minutes ago and was not so thrilled about now.

It was past the agreed time and he hadn't rung her. Hopefully he had been held up somewhere too, or he'd decided he wouldn't answer the phone when she'd tried to ring him. It was the sort of pathetic thing he would do. There was nothing else she could do but ring for help— and the only person she could ring was Simon. Maybe they could get the bike upright before Mick came.

Simon had walked swiftly around to his father's house and cornered Mia in the kitchen to ask what she knew about Tara's due clients. Still concerned about the idea that one of Tara's birthing women might have a less than salubrious home life, he couldn't settle until he'd been reassured.

But Mia's comment that after her last birth Tara's only due woman was Maeve, had him thrust back into confusion.

So it couldn't be a premature labour because she'd be telling that woman to come for transfer. Which meant only one thing. She'd lied to him. To his face. And he couldn't think of one damn good reason why she'd had to do that.

And then his phone rang. 'Hello?'

'Simon?' It was her.

His hand tightened on the phone as he waved to Mia before he walked back towards the manse. 'Tara? Are you okay?'

Tara's 'Not really...' made his heart rate jump. 'What happened?'

'I came off my bike and I can't stand it up. I need help.'

'Where are you?' He looked up at Mia and pointed towards the manse. Mia nodded and waved him away.

There was a pause. 'I'm sorry about the dinner.'

He brushed that aside. 'Where are you?'

'On the old rubbish dump road.'

He hadn't thought there were any houses down that way. 'And you're all right? You're not hurt?'

'Pride's pretty banged up, my ankle is tender, but physically I'm scratched, that's all.'

He tried to hold them back but the words came out anyway. 'What are you doing out there?'

She sighed. 'It's a long story. I'll tell you when you get here. Turn onto the rubbish tip road and I'm about a kilometre in on the left just as you hit the low part of the road. Watch out for the loose gravel,' she added dryly.

'Twenty minutes!' And it had better be a good reason because he didn't like any of the ones he'd come up with.

CHAPTER FOURTEEN

'SIMON WILL BE here in time. He'll be here.' The words echoed eerily in the encroaching dusk and Tara huddled further into her thin top. It was summer, for pity's sake, and she hadn't had the forethought to bring warmer clothes, but down in the hollow the mist was cool. That's what happened when you forgot the way of the world.

She'd fallen into this trap s-o-o-o many times before you would think she'd have learnt her lesson. Why would Simon Campbell, darling of his two families and, in fact, all of Lyrebird Lake, forgive her for lying to him?

Especially when he didn't understand the reason.

Maybe the fault did lie a little with her. Come on, Tara, a lot with her. She didn't trust him enough to give him the tools to believe her. Hadn't let him into her dilemma because she'd been too afraid he'd turn away from her. So she'd lied instead.

Self-sabotage or what? If she was honest, somewhere in the back of her head the voices had been saying he would let her down. Maybe that was why she'd made this tryst so difficult.

Well, she was in trouble now. It was getting dark, miles from anywhere, and she didn't want to think about the possibility that she'd put her heart on the line again to be broken.

She lifted her chin. She wasn't some twelve-year-old orphan sent on her way. She was a grown woman. A grown professional woman and she would get over this just as soon as she figured a way to get back to civilisation, and she may as well start now because he wasn't going to come.

Then headlights crossed the tops of the trees and in the distance she heard an echo of a car roaring up the hill.

'Simon,' she whispered, and the words floated into the darkness. Now that he was coming, she dreaded seeing the disgust on his face. She'd let him down with her lies but she hadn't been able to think of anything else she could do to prevent her world crumbling. He'd probably think she was leaving with Mick. She may as well. There was nothing here for her now.

But it wasn't Simon. It was Mick. Towing a trailer behind a disreputable old sedan. Tara's heart sank and she considered throwing herself back into the bushes so he wouldn't see her, but it was too late.

He pulled up in a shower of gravel because he'd been driving far too fast as usual. She should have known it wasn't Simon with the car engine screaming up the hill in the dimness.

'Where's the bike?' The words flew out of his mouth as fast as Mick got out of the car. He looked around suspiciously.

Tara sighed. She'd forgotten how childish he was. 'I lost it in the gravel so it's in the bush behind me.'

'Is it okay?'

'What about me?'

'Oh, yeah. You okay?' But his eyes were scanning the bush and he was on his way before she could answer.

'Fine,' she said to his back, and decided Mick was dumb enough and strong enough not to ask for help to extricate the bike.

She glanced up the road and wished like hell she'd never rung Simon. She considered phoning him back and saying, *Don't come. I'll be home soon.* Except that would involve more explanations and possibly more lies. She'd lied enough. All she could do was hope Mick would load the bike and go as soon as possible.

Mick did manage to get the bike on the trailer before Simon arrived but that was where Tara's luck ran out.

Simon turned off the main road and frowned at the deserted gravel road that stretched ahead in the dimness. He switched on his headlights and slowed right down. She'd said about a kilometre. Something was going on. And he was pretty sure he wasn't going to like it. But he was surprisingly unworried about that. Lots of people did things he didn't like and he got over it. Look at his parents lying to him. Look at Maeve. Though he hadn't got over Rayne's part in that. But this would be okay. Right.

Anyway, he loved Tara and the fact that she'd rung him for help was a big plus.

But he would be much happier when he found her and could see for himself she was unhurt.

And then he saw her. Standing in the gloom at the side of the road beside a dirty sedan and a trailer with her bike on the back. She must have found someone to help her get it home.

Well, that was one problem solved. She was standing, and apart from a limp when she came towards where he parked she looked okay. Thank goodness.

Then he saw the driver of the vehicle and his brows rose. Even in the poor light he could see the heavy tattoos and plaited beard. Noted Tara's guarded stance as he pulled up and climbed out of his vehicle. Thank goodness he'd hurried. The situation was not what he'd expected but as long as Tara was okay...

Mick waved him away. 'We don't need help, mate.'

Simon ignored him. 'You okay, Tara?' He crossed to her side, all the while noting the smudges of blood through the slits in her jeans, the abrasions on her arms and the extreme wariness on her face. He wanted to hug her but she was sending keep-off vibes like a missile launcher, telling him to stay away, and he frowned. 'How's the ankle?'

Mick lifted his head at that and took a step towards Simon. Towered over him. 'Who are you?'

Simon looked him up and down. Remained supremely unconcerned that he was outweighed. He'd faced down bigger men than this guy, and knew how not to antagonise. Usually. 'I'm a friend of Tara's. Who are you?'

'Mick. Me and Tara grew up together. We don't need your help.'

He smiled at Mick. 'Good to meet you, Mick. Then you'll understand if I ask Tara that.' He didn't wait for Mick's answer. 'Tara?'

'Ankle's fine. Sore but I can walk.' Tara was looking worried and he wished he could tell her how skilled he was at managing stroppy people. He was the one they called if a husband lost the plot in his concern for his wife. Though he wasn't feeling his usual detached self as he took in the full magnificence of this quite obnoxious guy, making ownership moves towards Tara.

'It's nice of you to take Tara's bike home for her.'

Mick laughed. 'Yeah. But it's my home. My bike. She gave it back.' He leered. 'I was thinking I might take Tara, too.'

Simon fought down his sudden out-of-character urge to knock the guy's teeth in and looked at Tara.

'And how does Tara feel about that?'

She glared at Mick. 'You've got the bike. Let's go, Simon.'

Simon did a double-take. 'You're giving him the bike?'

Tara straightened. To Simon she ground out, 'It's mine to give.' To Mick, 'I want you out of my life. Merry Christmas.'

Tara walked away from them both, climbed into Simon's car and slammed the door. She stared straight ahead, ignoring them, though her eyes were squinting sideways in the side mirror as she tried to catch a glimpse of what was happening. She'd had the desperate idea if she left they'd both look stupid if they started something, and she didn't think even Mick would drag her out of her chosen car with force. She was right.

Simon opened the car door just as Mick's car started up and drove ahead to find somewhere to turn around.

'What the hell was that all about?'

'Can we just turn the car around and get out of here first? Please!'

Simon reversed the car with very uncharacteristic roughness and speed, and they skidded away from the fateful corner in a shower of gravel, much like Mick's arrival. Tara sighed.

'Don't you sigh at me. What the hell were you thinking? You arranged that. Didn't you? To meet this man in a dark and deserted place, to hand over the bike. By yourself. After lying to me so I wouldn't demand to come with you.'

She looked at him. His face was set. His lips compressed. Those strong shoulders were rigid with disbelief. She'd done that to him. Hurt him. Made him uncharacteristically angry. Knocked herself off the pedestal she'd been trying to balance on. 'You're right. That just about covers it.'

'No, that doesn't just about cover it.' They turned off the road and onto the Lyrebird Lake road and Simon pulled over. Switched the engine off. They sat there for a few seconds and Tara gathered her thoughts. Behind them Mick's lights turned towards Sydney and disappeared. She guessed she did owe Simon an explanation but she wasn't happy with his high-handed tone or the fact that this had all backfired on her. She'd been trying to do the right thing but she'd had nowhere to go. She had lied to Simon.

So she gave it to him straight. No wrapping. It was all a mess now anyway. 'Mick wanted the bike back. He's not pleasant when he's in this mood. I didn't want him to upset anyone in Lyrebird Lake so I'd rather just give it to him.'

'So you arranged to meet him out here? On your own?'

She shrugged. 'I'm not afraid of Mick. He looks worse than he is but I didn't want him being horrible in front of Louisa.' She looked up at him. 'Or Maeve, or Mia.'

She sighed again. Almost defiantly. 'Or you.'

That just inflamed him more. 'And how were you going to get home after you handed this man your only possession?'

'Walk.'

'That's beautiful.' He grimaced in the darkness. 'Walk. On a dark road. What is it, four miles?' His hands tightened on the steering-wheel until his knuckles were white. Despite the quietness of his tone Tara could tell he was furious. 'You put yourself in danger. All the time.'

He shook his head. Flabbergasted as he ran

over it in his mind. 'There's the motorbike I was getting used to, the controlled risk of skydiving. I get that, I really do. But then there's being wilfully, personally risky, meeting substance-affected men in deserted places at night. I can't believe you didn't ask me for help.'

'No. I didn't.'

He glared at her. 'Instead of telling me the truth, accepting my help and being safe?'

She shrugged. 'I'm used to looking after myself. I thought I would be safe.'

'See, now I have an issue with that.'

'I rang you in the end.'

'Far too little too late. Maybe we have rushed into this. Or maybe I have. This morning I would have sworn we had a future together but I'm not so sure now. If there's one thing I won't put up with it's being shut out and lied to, especially by someone I l—um…someone I care deeply for!'

Someone he cared deeply for. And she'd spoiled it all.

Tara risked a glance at him and he was staring straight ahead as if the road was going to open up and swallow them at any moment. She almost wished it would.

The silence was loaded with regret on both sides but neither of them seemed to be able to break it. It took for ever to get back to the empty manse.

Then they were home. Everyone else was at Mia's and as Simon helped her in she wondered if he'd go to the family dinner now. But he didn't say anything, just appeared with the cotton wool and disinfectant and bathed her cuts, despite the fact she wanted him to just leave her alone.

Ushered her to bed. But there was a huge distance between them of things that were said and unsaid as he closed her door and left her. On both sides.

CHAPTER FIFTEEN

TARA OPENED HER eyes at six o'clock on Christmas Eve morning and lay in her bed, staring at the ceiling full of ghosts from Christmas past, even though she didn't want to.

Long-gone children's faces, long-gone empty dormitories, less-than-wonderful foster-parent experiences. And all those Christmas Eves full of expectations. Well, she didn't have any of those today after last night.

She'd lost the one man who could have rounded out her world. She sat up and hugged her pillow to her chest.

Simon had been right. She should have faced the music earlier rather than later. Discussed her concerns rationally with the man who cared and had been nothing but supportive. She had a sudden memory of their morning with the breech birth. How safe she'd felt because Simon had been there. How supportive he'd been without being authoritative. How proud he'd been of her ability to understand what had needed to be done and doing it.

She'd thrown away her chance with Simon and today was going to be a long, long day of tragedy of lost opportunities.

She should have trusted him to understand. She just didn't know how to trust people. Another hard, painful lesson learned. It was too late for her and Simon but she vowed she would try in the future.

But for now she needed to make sure she didn't spoil anyone else's day.

Apart from Simon hating her, today was going to be a good day. She would smile and play cheerful families one last time. She'd let go of the silly pipe dream of happily ever after with Simon that she should never have contemplated.

He'd be gone soon and she'd see if she could settle back into the world of Lyrebird Lake. If she couldn't settle then what she'd learnt here would hold her in good stead for the future.

Starting from now, she needed to appreciate the fact that she could hear the cicadas in the tree outside her window. Savour the warmth that was already creeping into the morning. Sniff the air with the enticing fragrance of baking that had hung over the house like an aromatic fog for the last two days. Go outside onto the springy kikuyu grass and watch the nodding reindeer and manger animals gyrate as the sun rose.

Then she'd be ready for what today would bring and what it wouldn't bring.

The feeling of just-out-of-reach simple pleasures drew her out of bed. Today would have to look after itself and she would savour every moment because that was all she had control over.

There was a tinkle of music and she even

managed a tiny, crooked smile into her pillow before she put it back on her bed. Louisa had the Christmas music on again. Maeve would be so glad tomorrow when it would be gone. Her eyes stung as she thought about losing Maeve as a friend and then pushed that thought too back into her mind.

She scooted down the hallway with her clothes under her arm. Ten minutes later she let herself out the front door into the misty morning light to start the day on her own. Build her walls of serenity so no one could see the lost little girl inside her.

Except that Simon was there on the seat in front of the manger. She almost turned around and ran back to her room—but instead she lifted her chin. Better to do this when no one else was there.

Simon felt some of his tension ease as Tara came across the grass. At least she was going to talk to him. 'Merry Christmas Eve, Tara.'

Her face said she didn't think so and his own interpretation said that was his fault. He'd done so many things wrong.

'Merry Christmas Eve, Simon.' She sat with a gap he could have driven a car through between them.

When he looked sideways at her a tiny silver tear slid out of her eye and rolled down her cheek, and he thought his heart would break. 'Don't cry.'

She brushed it away. 'I'm not.' Sat up straighter and rubbed her face.

'Baby Jesus arrives at midnight tonight.'

She looked at him and frowned. And then he could see she imagined a tiny beautifully wrapped doll all tucked up in straw.

'That will be awesome.'

They sat there looking at the space for a physical sign of a new beginning and miraculously he saw the signs of her glimpsing that maybe there was still a chance of a new beginning between them too.

He shifted along the seat and closed the gap between them on the bench, and all the motorised animals nodded.

'You okay?' His hand came across and picked up her fingers. Squeezed them in his. For a few seconds she just let it lie there in his palm and he squeezed her fingers again gently until she returned the pressure.

'I guess you did come to save me.'

'I was later than I wanted to be. You need to learn to trust me.'

She looked down at their hands and then back at his face. 'You need to learn to trust me. I've looked after myself for a lot of years.'

He sighed. She was right. 'I thought I did but then things happened and I lost it again. I'm sorry.'

She smiled at that, a little mistily, and looked away.

He'd better be able to fix this because looking at her face and not kissing her was killing him. 'I'm sorry I was horrible to you last night.'

'You were horrible to me.'

Well, that didn't go as planned, he thought regretfully.

'But I can see why you were.' She straightened her shoulders. 'And I'm sorry I lied to you.'

She was so brave. His Tara. 'You did lie to me. But I can see why you did.'

She nodded in the morning light. 'I didn't want you to meet Mick.'

He smiled ruefully at that. 'I didn't really want to meet Mick either. But I do want you to lose the ridiculous idea that any obnoxious person who comes looking for you is going to affect the way we feel about the Tara we know and care about. You have the whole of Lyrebird Lake behind you. Mick needs to see that. You need to see that.'

He looked at her under her brows. 'And he's not getting your bike.'

'I don't care about the bike.'

'I do. It's yours. I've given his number plate to the police and told them if he gives it back we won't press charges. They checked and it's your name on the paperwork.'

He saw her look of cautious hope but she said again, 'I don't care about the bike. What if he comes back? He can be very aggressive.'

He shook his head. Not the answer. 'Giving him the bike won't stop that. If he comes back we make him welcome. There must have been a reason he was your friend.

'But Mick's really not the bad man here. I am. Can you forgive me? For being angry?' He shook his head. 'I'm having a hard time forgiving myself. I never lose it.'

'You lost it.' She was teasing him now. Typical. 'Pretty controlled kind of guy, eh?' And he deserved it.

'I thrive on it. Usually. Like to have my world lined up and the bases covered.' He glanced at her. It was always good to look at Tara. 'Do you know why I lost it?'

She nodded. 'You were worried about me?'

'That too. But mainly because I've just discovered if I lose you I lose everything.'

He could see she didn't know how to answer that. All he could hope for was that when she did figure it out he'd like the answer.

Finally she did. 'I didn't want you to meet Mick in case I lost you.'

Now, that was good to hear. She did care and she squeezed his hand and turned towards him. A fresh, beautiful, Christmas Eve morning face with far less shadows than it had had a few minutes ago. 'Thank you for understanding, Simon. It's just that he can be very intimidating.'

'So can you.'

She shook her head. 'You're not intimidated by me.'

He had to laugh at that. He who had a burning question he couldn't ask.

'Tara.'

'Yes, Simon?'

'Do you love me?'

She looked away. Then back at him and her face seemed to glow. Even he could see that. His heart leapt. 'I might.'

She was so brave. Braver than him. Thank the stars for that. Time for him to be brave. 'Will you kiss me?' He puckered his lips. She looked at him like he was mad.

'No.'

'Please.'

She leaned over and did a reasonable job considering they were out in the street.

Fearless woman. Yep, there was love in that. He could feel his heart lift and swell and he just wanted to crush her to him. Finally he said it. 'Tara. I absolutely, one hundred percent, irrevocably love you.'

She blinked and chewed those gorgeous lips, and slowly an incredulous and painfully disbelieving smile grew on her beautiful mouth.

He didn't stop while he was ahead. 'And I want to marry you. As quickly as I can because you've spent too much of your life alone and, despite all my dozens of relatives, I've been alone too.'

She nodded. Quite vigorously. Apparently dumbstruck but he could work with that.

'But I need to marry you mostly because I love you, you crazy, adventurous woman.'

She swallowed and it must have helped because finally she said the words he wanted to hear.

'And I love you too, you too-sane, too-careful, too-bossy and will-learn-to-be-adventurous, man.'

She leaned over and kissed him again but this time he took over. Kissed her so thoroughly they forgot where they were until Maeve called from the veranda, 'Hey, you two. Come inside and do that.'

They broke apart and Simon was glad it was still too early for the neighbours to be around.

Tara grinned as Maeve turned and went back into the house. Asked thoughtfully, 'Just how many relatives have you got?'

'We have two sets. Which, now that I come to think of it, is perfectly designed for us.'

She wasn't really taking this in. She was gazing more at the love that was dusting her as it radiated from Simon. The way he looked at her, held her hand as if it was the most precious hand in the world. Hers?

She let the words resonate. 'Perfectly designed? How so?'

His eyes met hers with an exuberance she couldn't help smiling at. 'We have our Lyrebird Lake family, your new mama, Mia...' he grinned at that '...and Angus as dad. He's a very cool dad to come on late in life, let me re-assure you there.'

Tara knew that but she loved the way Simon was painting the picture. His pleasure at this the most precious gift he could share with her, his family, and her heart felt like it was open-ing like a flower starved of sunlight. One petal at a time.

'You'll have a new grandmother in Louisa, who will be over the moon. And will sew beau-tiful blankets for our children.' This was said smugly.

Louisa would be her grandmother. A huge lump rose into her throat with that incredible thought.

But Simon had only started as he kept adding depth to the picture. 'And two new little sisters in Layla and Amber, who I hope you will con-sider as bridesmaids. They look very pretty all dressed up. And Maeve will want to be maid of honour.'

She hadn't even thought about a wedding but suddenly she realised she would have one of those too. And sisters-in-law of her own.

So much to take in, to get used to, to be nervous about even.

But while the joy of a family would be hers, it was nothing compared to the thought of waking up beside Simon in the morning, every morning, and going to bed at night together for the rest of their lives. Spending their lives together. Everything was a wonderful, amazing Christmas tree of bonuses on top of everything. And Simon was her shining, love-filled star.

But he hadn't finished. 'And for your other family, we'll met the sisters and then we'll fly to America. See my dad and mum—it might take a while, but you'll grow to love her. Totally different from Mia, and she has fabulous taste because she thinks the sun shines out of me.'

He looked quite satisfied at that and she

laughed. 'Imagine that. I think you're going to be quite a needy husband.'

His eyes darkened. 'I love the thought of being your husband. And I am needy. I need you because I've finally found what's been missing in my life. You're my heart, my love, my future. I look at you and feel the smile shine inside me like Louisa's blue star.'

'I'm your blue star.' He could see she liked that. Good.

'Shining at me as you save me. I love you, Tara.'

Tara could feel tears prickle and swallowed them back. The thought floated across her mind that Simon wouldn't mind her tears, she didn't have to hold back anything, or hide anything, or wait for anything. Simon knew all about her, warts and all, the only person who really did, and he was here and still loved her, and maybe everything that had gone before had been preparing her for this moment.

'I know you said you didn't expect evermore. But I wish you would. Stay with me for ever.'

Yes, please. 'And beyond.' They, she and Simon, were the future. She could see it and it was magic.

'And we are having a wedding cake with candles.'

She blinked and looked back at him. 'What? You can't have candles on a wedding cake.'

He lifted his chin and she recognised the tiny streak of stubbornness that stopped him from being perfect. Thank goodness he wasn't perfect. 'It's our cake. We can have what we want. And on our anniversary every year we'll have a cake with candles, and including your birthday, when you will definitely have candles, in twenty years' time you'll have blown out the same number of candles as everyone else in your life.'

'You're crazy.'

'About you.'

'And I am crazy about you, Simon Campbell.'

'Mrs Campbell.'

'Not yet.'

And suddenly he was serious. Intent. 'I love you, Tara. I'm not blind. I know we'll have our disagreements but I love the woman inside you. The survivor. The nurturer who has never had a chance to share that gift of nurturing. Share it with me, with the children I can't wait to have with you. We're going to have so much fun with our children.'

He was serious again. 'I can't wait to buy the toys you never had.' She could feel her frown but he'd known it was coming. 'Before you fire up, it's not pity, it's love. I can't wait to play the games you never played—with you, when we play with our children. And I know I'm going to love you more every single day. In fact, even thinking about this is driving me crazy. This has to happen as quickly as I can arrange it.'

She laughed. 'We have to finish Christmas first.'

'Yes, we'll have Christmas, our first Christmas together. And Maeve will have her baby. But inside, when all the revelry is around us, I'll know that you are my future. And ahead is a whole life of joy and adventure with you.'

He took her hand and drew her to her feet. 'Thank you, Tara.' He stroked her face and his eyes were solemn as he stared down into her face. 'My Christmas is here because you have given me your love and that is the greatest gift I could ever wish for.'

* * * * *